Mammoths at the Gates

BOOKS BY NGHI VO

Siren Queen

The Chosen and the Beautiful

THE SINGING HILLS CYCLE

The Empress of Salt and Fortune

When the Tiger Came Down the Mountain

Into the Riverlands

Mammoths at the Gates

Mammoths
at the
Gates

NGHI VO

TOR PUBLISHING GROUP
NEW YORK

This is a work of fiction. All of the characters, organizations, and events portrayed in this novel are either products of the author's imagination or are used fictitiously.

MAMMOTHS AT THE GATES

A Tordotcom Book
Published by Tom Doherty Associates / Tor Publishing Group
120 Broadway
New York, NY 10271

www.tor.com

Tor® is a registered trademark of Macmillan Publishing Group, LLC.

The Library of Congress Cataloging-in-Publication Data is available upon request.

ISBN 978-1-250-85143-7 (hardcover)
ISBN 978-1-250-83800-1 (ebook)

Our books may be purchased in bulk for promotional, educational, or business use. Please contact your local bookseller or the Macmillan Corporate and Premium Sales Department at 1-800-221-7945, extension 5442, or by email at MacmillanSpecialMarkets@macmillan.com.

First Edition: 2023

Printed in the United States of America

0 9 8 7 6 5 4 3 2 1

to the Mulroney family

Mammoths at the Gates

Chapter One

"—and that was how we got the moon back up the mountain and into the sky, and no one was ever the wiser. You can tell it was us because when you see the moon's face turned out fully, the dark marks are where the youngest sister kissed her before she said goodbye."

The woman steering the cart winked and tapped her lips, painted a dark and shiny green-black, and Chih made another note in their book, both the end of the story and that the woman's lip paint hid darker marks underneath, visible only when one was close enough to see.

Tattoos, maybe, or very fine scarification? Is there a good way to ask without being rude?

Chih was still pondering the question when the woman nodded, pulling her team of oxen to a halt.

"And here we are, cleric. This is where I turn north, and you shift for yourself."

"Oh, thank you! I'm sorry, I was listening to your story, and I missed the signs."

Chih climbed down from the wagon, dragging their pack with them and settling it on their shoulders. They turned to bow their thanks formally, but the woman peered over their shoulder towards the path behind them, less a road than a foot-track into the sparse woods.

"I would have missed it myself if the road hadn't widened to a turnaround. This is some desolate country you all have here in the west. Where did you say you were headed again?"

Chih couldn't help smiling, not when they were so close, when the earth smelled right and the cicadas filled the air with a thunderous buzz. In another few weeks, the cicadas would all be dead, and the novices would sweep up drifts of golden husks to be crushed and added to the compost bins.

I made it back in time for the cicadas, they thought.

"I'm going home to the Singing Hills abbey," they said.

From the Red Road, it was another day's walk to the abbey gates. Properly, it was closer to a day and a half, but Chih knew that there was a warm bed, food, and family waiting for them at the end, and they pushed on through the thinning light. They knew these woods, and while there was no such thing as a safe wilderness, they knew its dangers: candle ghosts and echo spirits that would lead them in circles, shy wolves that could grow hungry.

Cleric Pan would say that this is exactly how you get led into the woods and eaten by a wolf, but Cleric Pan also told us that the castle at Keph-Valee can lift from its foundations and fly. It probably can't, and I probably won't be eaten by a wolf either.

Still, it had been four years since they had last made this trip. Once they almost mistook a deer track for the path, and once they heard the voice of the Divine calling to them for help. Home was still home, they thought as they walked, and it was a mistake to let nostalgia convince them that it was completely safe.

The deer track had cost them some time, however, and the sun was below the horizon when they broke the treeline to the plains. Across the rolling green, they could see the walls of the Singing Hills abbey, ancient and scarred with the marks of old conflicts, and so beloved that it made Chih's heart hurt.

They sniffled a little, and then they blinked when they saw a pair of dark shapes before the twin timber gates.

Are they . . . did they build sheds on the green? Did a traveling show or a weapons dealer arrive with their covered wagons for some reason?

Then one of the dark shapes moved, its lumbering gait and the round shape of its head unmistakable. It turned so it stood fully in the dying light of the day and uncurled its short trunk to arch back like a snake against its head before it bellowed, a shrill trumpeting sound that carried to where Chih stood and beyond, likely all the way back to the Red Road.

Mammoth, Chih thought, frozen. *Mammoths at the gates.*

Chapter Two

From the treeline, Chih paced and thought about what they should do, what they *could* do. They could turn around and try to find out what was going on from the town up the river. They could try the postern gate, which was less a secret than it was simply inaccessible, hidden along the ridge, a relic of the time when the abbey actually had been a real military fortification.

I heard there was the cave-in a few years ago, they meant to dig it out, but did they ever? I could try it—

Chih's head jerked up at a low hooting: two slurred hollow notes, the second higher and softer. It was as familiar as their own face, and they turned with relief and no small amount of joy.

The hoopoe in the tree behind them was male by his bright coloration and larger than most of the neixin that lived in the Singing Hills aviary, almost the size of a crow or a young chicken. He gazed down at Chih curiously from his perch in the tree, twisting his head back and forth.

"Well, well," he said. "What a time for you to make your way home."

"Cleverness Himself! Yes, I seem to have chosen a bad time, haven't I?"

"Never a bad time to come home. I'm happy to see you. You need a haircut."

Chih passed a hand over the two inches of hair on their head, grinning in spite of themselves.

"The barber in the last town I was in ran off with the circus. I did try."

"*Try harder!*" the bird barked in a perfect imitation of Cleric Hahn, who had once been a drill instructor in Wen, and Chih laughed.

"I can ask someone to take care of it for me when I get inside the walls—that is, if I can get inside the walls?"

Cleverness Himself whistled, a disdainful sound.

"Oh, you want to get in? There's nothing easier. Will you stand me a ride?"

"Oh, of course."

Chih lifted their left shoulder slightly in invitation, and Cleverness Himself glided down to secure his perch, his sharp nails knitting through the fabric of their indigo robe. He was heavier than Almost Brilliant, and his bulk actually blocked their vision on one side, but then they both got the balance.

"Tsk, all this and you've lost weight too," Cleverness Himself said disapprovingly, flexing his feet on their shoulder. "Let's get you inside so we can start feeding you up again."

"Rice porridge and rice porridge and rice porridge, and maybe a slice of toasted tofu if we've all been good," said Chih with a sigh. "Where am I going?"

"Home, of course. Start walking."

Chapter Three

To Chih's uneasy surprise, Cleverness Himself marched them down to the plain, over the footbridge that crossed the creek, and then straight among the cluster of small blue-and-white-striped pavilions that they had missed when they were staring at the mammoths in surprise. Planted at the center of the pavilions was a pole bearing an embroidered flag, that of a hound with a broad chest and a tiny curly tail facing right, one paw up.

"That's the flag of Northern Bell Pass, isn't it?" asked Chih, and Cleverness Himself whistled disdainfully.

"It surely is. More precisely, with its little paw up like that, it's the insignia of the Coh clan. Cute little dog, don't you think? Who's got a cute little face? Who's got the most adorable little paws?"

The last was uttered more loudly, pitched to carry, and suddenly there was a tall woman striding towards them out of the dim early evening. Her long robes looked too light for the evening chill and too long for the outdoors, dragging in the grass. Despite that, she moved with an easy and menacing athleticism. Her head was half-shaved, one side as clean as a cleric's, the other side braided back to fall in long tails over her shoulder. By her side there was a long and slender sword of the ceremonial sort often used as a pointer, though Chih had the sinking sensation that for this woman, a stabbing weapon was a stabbing weapon.

"Keep a civil tongue in that beast's head, cleric, or I will cut it out," she snapped, and Chih hurriedly bowed. What a welcome home.

"Forgive us," they began, but Cleverness Himself shifted to the top of Chih's head, puffing up indignantly.

"A beast, really! You know better than that, that I am no beast. I am a neixin of Singing Hills, upon whose lands you are currently trespassing."

The woman's sharp eyes shifted to Cleverness Himself, which would have been more of a relief if the hoopoe wasn't actually standing on Chih's head.

"I am an advocate of the empire, escorted by a detachment of the southern regiment and traveling on legal business. There is no land on this continent where I am a trespasser."

"Wrong again," Cleverness Himself trilled. "Singing Hills stands on old promises made by greater than any you have ever spoken with, and it will stand long after *you* are gone."

Something about that pricked the woman's anger—Chih could almost feel it shift, and they spread their hands out placatingly even as they shifted one foot back to dodge or to run.

"I am Cleric Chih of Singing Hills," they started hurriedly. "I've been traveling, and I am only trying to return—"

"Then return," the woman said shortly. "And take your bird from this place before it says something you both have cause to regret."

Chih could actually feel Cleverness Himself getting ready to make some potentially fatal response to that, and before he could do so, they reached up to grab him off their head and hug him to their chest. Despite his size, he still felt delicate in their grasp, his heart buzzing like a thousand flies, and they were careful not to crush him even as they bowed again.

"Impolite!" Cleverness Himself growled, pecking hard at Chih's hands, and it was, as rude as grabbing another cleric and covering their mouth.

"Still alive," Chih hissed in response. "Now I'm getting out of here before—"

"You can come this way," said another voice, and Chih squeaked in surprise, letting go of Cleverness Himself who exploded out of their grasp and flapped hard in shock at the person who had gotten too close without either of them noticing.

The other person fell back, letting Cleverness Himself make a tight circle before landing on Chih's shoulder again.

"Now who in the world are you?" he asked sternly.

The newcomer was a woman perhaps five or so years

younger than Chih themself, dressed more simply than the other, but with the same hooded eyes and sharp features. Where the former had been stern, however, this woman was cheerful, with a wide mouth that seemed inclined to smile and a patch of skin on her chin and her throat that was paler by far than the rest, ragged at the edges and leading up to her cheeks with island-specks of white.

"Vi In Yee," she said by way of introduction. "I was introduced when we first showed up, but there was a lot going on that morning."

"Corporal Vi In Yee?" asked Chih, who had noticed the beaded braid of red mammoth fur coiled into a circle and pinned to her shoulder.

"Ha, yes, corporal, that's correct. You've had some dealings with the mammoth corps, then?"

"Some," Chih allowed, falling into step. "Though I have to say that I have never seen you so far south."

"Oh, we don't like it much. It makes everyone cranky and tired, riders and mammoths both. Still, we get on all right. This time of year is better for it than some."

Chih almost missed a step when they realized that Vi In Yee was leading them to the two mammoths that stood by the tall gate. Neither was saddled, and they were not tethered either, which Chih knew would allow them to come at a call or a whistle from the woman by their side.

"Come here," Vi In Yee said, walking forward. "Come meet them. That is, unless you are afraid."

Cleverness Himself whistled mistrustfully, but he

hopped down to Chih's shoulder again. His nails were sharp, and Chih had the idea that he wanted to spread a sheltering wing over them both, for all the good that would do.

"It would be an honor," Chih said firmly, and it was the truth. They had met mammoths before in their travels in the north, and they knew very well that the only harm in a well-trained mammoth came at the command of their rider.

Even knowing that, there was something more than a little intimidating about walking up to such large animals, one the classic russet red and the other red with four showy white socks and a large white patch over her face that spread down to cover her trunk. They swung their trunks in a companionable way as Vi In Yee walked ahead, her hands open to pet first one and then the other.

"Hello, my good girls," she said, her voice different from when she had been speaking to Chih. "Look at how lazy you have grown in the south, hah? So lazy! Come here, cleric. You can pet Sho if you want. Bibi's still young, and more temperamental."

Chih approached slowly, aware of the two enormous heads swinging towards them. The patched mammoth, Sho, reached for them before they had even made it to Vi In Yee's side, her trunk knocking against Chih's chest and hips. Her motions dislodged Cleverness Himself, who fluttered up into the air before coming back down with a creative Hangdian curse.

"Oh, hello, Sho," said Chih, stroking her trunk as they had seen Vi In Yee do. "They're bigger than I thought they would be."

"You've seen the common breed, I expect," said Vi In Yee with a casual condescension. "These two girls, they're royal mammoths. This isn't even as big as they'll get."

Chih took in that information as Sho grumbled with pleasure at being petted. They had ridden along with a mammoth scout and her mammoth up north. Common mammoths were smaller, slimmer, and plenty dangerous when they were roused. They were deadly on the battlefield, especially in a familial herd, but it was the royal mammoths that were the line breakers, the ones that would shake the earth and break down iron gates and stone walls.

As if reading Chih's thoughts, Vi In Yee nodded, leaning against Bibi's leg as if she was at home on her own porch. The slight smile on her face never changed at all.

"Sho and I, we were at the fight down in the Laofeng marshes, you know, earlier this year. That was nasty. Four days, nonstop pushing through the fen, being eaten alive by mosquitoes and gnats and who knows what else. Poor Sho got bitten so much her eyes swelled almost shut."

She paused.

"Still we pushed through, and when we came to Hao Bi's fortress, we were so pissed we trampled it flat. Eight royal mammoths reduced that place to kindling in a count of sixty."

They'd brought the bandit Hao Bi to stand trial at the capital. He was the only one who had survived out of a cohort of almost eighty soldiers. Eight mammoths and a count of sixty. Chih swallowed hard, realizing in a different way how big Sho was, even as she stuck one of the mobile fingers of her trunk into their pack to search for treats.

"That sounds very impressive," they said as steadily as they could, and Cleverness Himself hissed softly by their ear.

"It is. Now I have kept you from home long enough, you should get inside."

She considered Chih a moment before continuing.

"You seem sensible," she said. "I try to be sensible too. I'm not always good at it, but I do try. But my sister's carrying a heavy load of cases for the throne, and back home, our grandmother died just two months ago, and our parents' generation is trying to figure out who's going to be running things for the next twenty years. It's a mess, you know?"

"I can imagine. I'm sorry for your loss."

"I appreciate it. My sister, though—she runs a little hot, you know? It seems like your head cleric, they do too. Maybe between the two of us, we can keep things civil. That might be for the best, don't you think?"

Chih managed to fish up a small smile, hoping Cleverness Himself could resist a caustic remark at that. The mammoths, as gentle as they were right this moment, were too big to allow much in the way of caustic remarks.

"Thank you for introducing me to Bibi and Sho, corporal," they said. "I'll be on my way."

The tall gates were closed and bolted, but they were usually only open for festival days and the big pilgrimages. It was stranger to see the small gate barred, the one where the clerics and the traders went day-to-day. Chih tugged on the steel pull, producing a deep brazen toll that summoned a teenage novice to glare out the peephole.

"Who is it?" they said mistrustfully, and Chih started to speak, but Cleverness Himself puffed up again.

"You know very well who I am," he said. "And this is Cleric Chih, back from abroad. Open this door at once."

Chih started to say that there was no need for that, but it got the door open, the novice behind it peering at Chih with wide eyes.

"Welcome home," they said belatedly. "Shall I send for someone to take your things?"

"No, thank you. I'm going to head straight to the administrative office before it gets too late."

They started to walk on, and then they remembered when they had been a novice on door duty, greeting the traveling clerics fresh back from the road and from adventures they could only dream of. Now they understood why those clerics from their childhood were so nonchalant about their travels—there was really a lot more waiting for the ferry and trudging in the rain than there was arguing with tigers or being chased by Rose Moon ghouls, but still. There had been tigers and ghouls.

"Actually, wait, just a minute."

Chih took off their pack, putting it on the ground to pull out a bag of milk candy from Ning. The candies were a soft ivory white, covered with a delicate rice paper wrapper that melted in the mouth, and the paper bag itself bore the picture of a famous puppet theater character, the Rat Bandit.

"Here. You can have this if you promise to share with your friends."

The novice nodded, torn between curiosity and being the kind of teenager who was excited about nothing, and Chih smiled.

"Hope you like them," they said before walking on.

"You're spoiling them," Cleverness Himself muttered disapprovingly.

"The traveling clerics used to spoil us too. When they go out, they'll spoil the next lot. It's a big circle."

As they made their way to the administrative office, however, they couldn't help thinking about the fairy-tale books that were sold in the north, the ones parents bought to entertain their children with tales of Princess Morningstar, the Rat Bandit, and King Whale. Every story ended with the tiny picture of a mammoth following the last line of text, because mammoths came at the end, after stories, after dynasties, after empires.

After abbeys too, Chih thought uneasily, and they

looked around at the walls that seemed through all their life to be the most solid things in the world.

The administrative office was typically helmed by one senior cleric and at least two, often three, clerics and whichever neixin might be spared and interested in the work. It took a phenomenal amount of record-keeping to maintain an organization that was frankly all about record-keeping, and the office often hummed along with a kind of desperate good cheer that it would never be able to catch up with the world, let alone keep up with it.

Tonight, however, the office was sunk in quiet, and the only person present was one of the lay sisters, a woman so old that she just blinked drowsily at Chih from her cot in the back before gesturing at the hooks where the room chits were kept and going back to sleep. Chih found a crate in which to deposit their stack of written documentation and took one of the room chits on their way out, their unease increasing.

Where is everyone?

The number of Singing Hills clerics fluctuated, with around half in the field and half at home at any one time. Some were posted permanently at the abbey, some were posted almost permanently away, but Chih couldn't think of a time when it had ever been this empty.

I'm going to drop off my things, and then I'm going straight to the aviary. Almost Brilliant will tell me what's going on.

They made their way to the dormitories, matching the character on their chit to the one painted on the room door. All of the rooms contained a bed with baskets underneath for various personal items, a washbasin, and a writing box loaded with supplies, but some previous tenant had hung up a rather bad ink drawing of a hoopoe in flight as well. The beak was too large, and the legs stuck out like barbecue skewers, but something about the homely drawing made Chih smile as they unpacked their things. Hoopoes meant home.

I really should have a wash before I go to the aviary. Probably have a bite to eat too, but I just need to see Almost Brilliant.

The sky was black when they stepped back outside, but the moon was almost full and rising. It was probably still early enough that the aviary wouldn't be asleep yet, and even if it was, perhaps the doorkeeper could be asked to—

Chih yelped as they were grabbed from behind and lifted halfway off their feet. They flailed for the ground, a half dozen panicked thoughts running through their head, starting with mammoth scouts and ending with ghouls, but then there was a laugh, low and bright and delighted.

"Reflexes like that, how in the hells haven't you gotten knifed yet?"

"Ru!"

Chih spun around to grapple the cleric standing behind them, throwing their arms around them and hugging tight. Ru was taller than they were, steadier with their cane than other people were on two feet, and hugging them was a little like hugging a friendly tree. Burying their face in Ru's robes, they smelled ink and paper and peppery muscle liniment so sharp it made them sneeze. Chih stepped back, giving them a quick poke in the bicep.

"Look at you! You're twice as big as when I was last home."

"Are you going to say how tall I've gotten too?"

"No, you're not tall, you've shrunk, you're positively tiny now. But oh, Ru, it's so good to see you. What in the world is going on?"

Ru winced.

"I take it you got a good eyeful of what was going on at the gate?"

"You mean the woman from the Northern Bell Pass and the two royal mammoths she's got with her? Yes, they were pretty hard to miss!"

"Observant as ever. Actually, it's good that you made it home now. Come on, we should talk."

Chih started to object because the neixin in the aviary tended to turn in early, but something about the unaccustomed serious look on Ru's face made them nod and fall into step. The familiar rhythm of Ru's steps and the tap of their cane was another reminder: they were home and they were with one of their favorite people in the world. Suddenly, Chih found themself resentful of the mammoths at the gate in a way they hadn't been before. Before, they were alarmed and afraid. Now they were almost angry that something had broken the pattern of home, let alone something as unnerving as war mammoths.

"Where is everyone? The office is empty, and I don't think I've seen more than four people since I got inside."

"Oh, well, that's the easy question. The royal engineers drained Snakehead Lake."

"Seriously?"

"The whole thing, took out the dam, the works. I guess they needed the water somewhere else, so they took it and left the town of Houshi uncovered for the first time in about three hundred years."

Chih's head spun at the image, the ancient towers of Houshi rising up from the murky water, and all the doors thrown open to the light and the air. The Emperor of Iron and Gall had ordered the flooding of the town so quickly that there were people who had never escaped, and now their bones were free to tell their secrets. There were clerics at Singing Hills who could read a lifetime in a single molar and half a tibia, and they must have had their calipers and their trowels packed the moment they heard.

"So how many—"

"Almost everyone who could travel. The Empress of Wheat and Flood has given us a dispensation to work for four months, provided that we do so under the supervision of the imperial censors. After that, they're running the water back in."

"And whatever survived the first torrent probably won't survive the second."

"Right. You should have seen it. It was like everyone stopped sleeping to pack, the Divine pulled in about every favor they could to get the trip outfitted, a literal brawl broke out over some old maps. It was probably the most excitement I've ever seen around here."

"Until the mammoths showed up?"

"Honestly, after all that, the mammoths were an anticlimax. They're really very quiet and docile."

"When they're not knocking down the walls of fortresses," Chih said impatiently. "Ru."

"Right."

Ru came to a halt, and Chih realized with a chill that they had come to the remembrance hall. The doors were carved with the little cats that guarded the path of the dead, and someone had left a long-burning taper on the step, scenting the air with beeswax and bitter dried marigolds.

"Cleric Thien died. Three weeks ago."

"Oh. Oh."

Chih swallowed, expecting a rush of tears or a cry or anything that wasn't opening their mouth like a fish and making that silly sound. The floor suddenly felt very far away, and Ru's face swam in front of their eyes as they blinked hard.

"Oh," they said again, and they didn't realize that their hands were clenched into fists until Ru took one up to work it loose, their fingers smoothing the back of Chih's hand until it relaxed, slowly and reluctantly.

"How?"

"A cough. They picked it up last year, and it never quite went away. When they went, they went fast, I promise you, and without pain. The infirmary saw to that. Myriad Virtues and I were with them every moment until the end."

Chih nodded. There were many places they had been where that would be reckoned a clean death, a quiet one in bed and attended by people who cared. It was something people offered as a comfort, but dead was dead, and the only comfort—one more word, one more touch—was impossible.

"Can I—?"

"Of course. I'll be out here. Take your time."

Chih took a taper from the jar by the door, lighting it from the one on the step, before stepping out of their sandals. They didn't turn as Ru briefly clasped their shoulder, and they were struck, as they entered, by a moment of childish disbelief.

Of course Cleric Thien could not be dead. It was silly to think that. Cleric Thien was as tall as the poplars that grew by the creek. They were born old. They were as much a part of Singing Hills as the aviary, the tall curtain wall, the garden beds that were made from the stone of ancient houses.

The remembrance hall was long and narrow, dark except for Chih's taper, for what could the dead hope to see?

At the head of the hall, the tilted table waited, but before they could approach, there was a rustle in one of the small antechambers off to the side.

"Hello? Who's there?"

Chih, oddly relieved to put the moment off a little longer, turned to bow to Cleric Yu-Ching, carrying their own taper and blinking sleepily through the dark.

"Cleric Yu-Ching, I—"

"Oh, my baby!"

Before Chih could say another word, Cleric Yu-Ching swept them up in a hard hug. They were only wearing a scanty silk sleeping robe, and when it slipped half off their shoulder, Chih found their nose pressed to the giggling demon tattooed on Cleric Yu-Ching's shoulder, the one with half a man in one hand and the other half in another.

"Are you all right? Oh, look at you, you're so skinny, what have you—oh, my poor little baby!"

Chih and Ru had always lived in dread of Cleric Yu-Ching's too-tight hugs and propensity for pinching them when they misbehaved, but now Chih hugged them back just as hard and buried their face in the rampaging demon on their shoulder.

"It's good to see you, elder," Chih said, but Cleric Yu-Ching waved them off.

"Oh, there's no one here," they said fussily, "I can just

be uncle, can't I? But you are back, and goodness, just in time."

"I am. I—" Chih's breath hitched in their chest, and for a moment, they thought they might break down into sobs. The only thing that kept them back from tears was knowing that if they did, they would set off Cleric Yu-Ching as well, and they managed a small smile instead.

"I am glad I made it back before the interment. And I am glad to see you as well, uncle."

Cleric Yu-Ching gave them another hug before stepping back. They were of an age with Cleric Thien, old enough that their tattoos had grown faded and tired, and their stretched and empty earlobes dangled loosely halfway down their neck.

"What a good child you have always been. I expect you have come to pay your respects. Do you want me to come with you? I'm sure old Thien wouldn't mind."

"No, I'll be fine. You should go back to sleep, uncle. If you stay up too late, the moon will be jealous of your beauty."

Cleric Yu-Ching dimpled prettily, and gave Chih's hand a last squeeze.

"Good and flattering child. Well, I'll return to bed then, but if you need me, just knock. It's just me and the old dead ones here at night, you know."

"Of course, uncle. Thank you."

Chih loved Cleric Yu-Ching and had missed them terribly, but there was a breath of relief when the door shut and they were alone again. Some things, they figured, they needed to do on their own, but as they made their way towards where the tilted table waited, they started to wonder about that. The hall was too quiet, the air too heavy as they stood below the dais.

The wrapped body on the table was as tall as Chih remembered, but so much narrower. Over the previous weeks, Cleric Yu-Ching would have desiccated Cleric Thien's body with a mixture of lime and salt, wrapped in a succession of tightening bandages. Now the final wraps were silk secured by small brass pins, and what was left of Cleric Thien would be installed in the catacombs, the latest of the archivists who had given their lives and their stories over to Singing Hills.

There was a pair of flat cushions on the ground, and Chih took their place cross-legged on one of them.

"You told me—" Chih began, and they shook their head at how foolish their voice sounded, how small and silly. They took a deep breath, and they tried again, as Cleric Thien had always told them they must.

"You told me that if I could make it all the way to our sister abbey in Tsu, I would see neixin with tails like widow's veils, and a mountain that roared where our hills sing songs. I'm planning to go next year. The passage is finally clear again after the war with Ue County ended. I'm going to go, and it's going to be wonderful and strange and scary, just like—just like you told me it would be."

They dashed their tears away with the back of their hand, sniffling hard. What was there to say? Everything and nothing, and either way, it was too late.

"You told us the best stories," Chih said finally, rising to their feet to bow as low as they could.

Cleric Thien's robes were folded neatly by, ready to be interred with them, and Chih stopped to bury their face in the cotton and wool. That was worse than the rest, because the robes still smelled like them, and the grief rose up like a tide. Chih let it rise, let it wash over the top of their head and into their mouth, their throat, and their lungs, and then it drained away, leaving them spent and exhausted as they stood straight and put the dead cleric's robes back.

When they reached the entrance again, Ru was seated on the step, eating melon seeds from a leaf packet.

"Here," they said, and Chih took a few listlessly, cracking them between their teeth to get at the tiny morsel inside the shell.

"All right?" asked Ru, and Chih shook their head.

"Anything I can do?"

Chi slipped their sandals back on. They started to say no, of course not, but then they remembered.

"I want to see Almost Brilliant," they said, and when they did, all of the sorrow over missing their friend mingled with the pain of losing Cleric Thien, and they burst into tears.

Chapter Four

"Sorry," Chih said finally.

"What, you think I didn't cry my eyes out when they died? Shut up."

Ru handed them a cloth, and Chih wiped their eyes and blew their nose.

"Will the Divine be able to come back for the interment?" they asked. "They were close."

"I've sent word along. I hope so. It's not that far to Snakehead Lake, but it will be a shock. Cleric Thien wasn't that sick when everyone left."

The aviary sat at the rear of the compound, hard up against the solid rock ridge that formed a portion of Singing Hills' walls. Despite decades of scrubbing, there were still black marks high up on the stone where an angry Anh emperor had burned the aviary to the ground, ushering in a century of exile for neixin and clerics alike. Unlike a conventional aviary, the top was completely open to the sky, and the carved wooden shutters were designed to preserve the neixins' privacy rather than keep them in. The aviary's footprint was sprawling, perhaps the largest single space in the abbey that was not the archives themselves, a clutter of polished tree limbs, perches, and nesting boxes that had been acquired over generations of care. An aviary of brass and mammoth ivory, gifted to the abbey by the Empress of Salt and Fortune herself, sat in pride of place among the nesting boxes, very much admired but seldom used for its resemblance to a cage. It was a lively place, home to some forty neixin at a time, depending on who had stayed and who went, and it was busy from dawn to dusk.

As they approached, Chih became aware of a low clamor, voices raised in what sounded like anger and fear. Outside the door, a lay sister with a particularly sour expression sat tending her lantern and her key.

"What's going on?" asked Ru, and she shook her head.

"I knocked to ask a while ago, but they only shouted at me to mind my own business," she said irritably. "They've been going for a while now."

A sudden anxiety grabbed at Chih's heart. They knew it was probably only because of the revelation of Cleric Thien's death, but suddenly they were terrified for Almost Brilliant.

"Please," they said, on the verge of begging. "Please, if you could only call for Almost Brilliant—"

They stared as Ru pulled a key out of their robes, unlocking the gate.

"Where did you get that?" they asked in surprise, but Ru was already pushing inside, and they hurried to follow, pausing only to light a spare candle from the lay sister's lamp.

The aviary's shadows were long and deep. There was no lighting inside because the neixin drowsed off at dusk, and there was plenty of light when they went to assist that researcher or that transcriptionist. Together, Chih and Ru followed the raised voices to the interior, away from the open space where fledglings tried their first flights and where the neixins' allotment of mealworms was usually scattered.

Towards the rear, a tangle of wood and rope provided the adult birds with more comfortable perches, and the clamor rose up like a thicket of sound.

"What in the name of Ha Tuyet's tits was she thinking? What could possibly be going on in her head that she would—" That was unmistakably Cleverness Himself's voice, in an outraged shout.

"Don't you shout about her like that! Do you think you are making anything better? Shut up!"

"Don't tell me to shut up! We all need answers!"

"What you need could just about top off the ocean, Cleverness Himself!"

Ru and Chih exchanged a look, and Ru pushed ahead, moving faster now and leaving Chih to trail along behind.

We really shouldn't, Chih thought. *This is private. We're meant to be invited, and we haven't been.*

Still they followed just a step behind Ru, because the

shouting was only getting louder, and there was an edge to it they had heard before, in crowds before they turned into mobs, in the chaos before some situation turned irrevocably bad, if not fatal.

The center of the aviary would have been pitch dark without Chih's candle, and they stood briefly apart from Ru so they could cast more light. They had been there before, but there was something cavernous about the space even if it was open to the air. The spars of wood rose up overhead, crossing and crisscrossing like the branches of forest trees, and the air was alive with the fluttering of furious wings and the sparks of dozens of black oildrop eyes.

"What's going on here?" Ru demanded, and suddenly every eye was on them.

"Who's *that*?"

"That's the kid they caught stealing that line of fish at the market, don't you remember? They cried like anything when they got caught and were made to sit alone at meals for a whole month."

"Oh, *that* one? Didn't they fail their Vinh language exam so badly they made old Cleric Ai retire?"

"Oh, *that* one . . ."

The trouble with having the neixin around, memory spirits with impeccable and bottomless recall, was that they never forgot anything, neither the rise of empires nor the childhood embarrassments that could haunt you many years later.

"Yes," Ru agreed. "And currently the acting head of the abbey, unless you all forgot."

A furious din went up, and Chih's eyes widened, both at the news and at the insult.

"Ru," they hissed, but Ru didn't turn around, instead glaring around at the flock.

"I'll ask again, what's going on?"

There was a whir of feathers as Cleverness Himself came to perch on Ru's shoulder, so puffed up he looked almost twice his usual size.

"Go look in the nesting box, the one in the lion's mouth. Go see for yourself," he said, pecking at Ru's ear. More than once, Chih had thought that Ru and Cleverness Himself deserved each other. Certainly no one else could stand them.

Ru turned their head to one side to keep Cleverness Himself from savaging their ear, and they nodded their head at Chih.

"Bring the candle."

"Of course, most Divine," Chih muttered, but they brought the candle along.

The lion turned out to be a piece of stone statuary, a western lion the size of a large pig. Its raised paw had been broken off long ago, and the fangs were smoothed over into short nubs, but the gaping mouth gave ample room for a nesting bird to raise a chick or two. There was the normal spill of straw and scraps from the lion's jaws, but there were no chicks or eggs inside. Instead it was a female hoopoe, lying with a kind of limpness to her body that made Chih's breath catch in their throat. It wasn't the resting posture of a healthy bird, and the pattern of stripes on her wings was so much like Almost Brilliant's that Chih nearly cried out. Then she turned and Chih saw that no, it was someone else.

"Myriad Virtues?" asked Ru tentatively.

Cleverness Himself glided from Ru's shoulder to the lion's head.

"Myriad Virtues, get up. It's the acting Divine," he said gruffly. "They want to see your madness."

For all of his anger, he entered the nest to give Myriad Virtues the support of his body as she roused herself. She moved stiffly but her eyes shone in the candlelight as she came to her feet, crouched into a puffed-out, defensive ball.

"Why, it's that child," she said, her voice thin and reedy. "Surely you are not old enough to be the Divine?"

"I am not," Ru agreed. "It'll be a long time before anyone's foolish enough to leave me in charge permanently. But Myriad Virtues, what has happened?"

For a moment, Chih thought that Myriad Virtues, the first neixin they had ever spoken to, Cleric Thien's companion since before they or Ru were ever born, would not respond. Then with a soft breath too small even to be a sigh, they stretched out a wing, and Chih bit the inside of their cheek so hard they tasted blood.

Even in the flickering candlelight, it was easy to see

that Myriad Virtue's flight feathers had been clipped, cut with ruthless precision almost down to the succeeding row of secondaries.

It's been done with some care. Someone did it with very sharp shears, and—and they are so even that she must not have struggled at all. How did she sit still for it?

"Who did this?" Ru said, their voice quiet.

"I did," Myriad Virtues said, her frail voice growing stronger. "Why, child, I did."

"We don't know who did it," Cleverness Himself said. "She came back like this after sunset. She can still fly just a little like that, but she walked back in. She *walked*—"

"Cleverness Himself, it is a wonder that you do not get tired of your own voice because I can tell you, the rest of us are weary to death of it!"

A third hoopoe swept into the lion's mouth, shoving Cleverness Himself out so hard that he dropped almost to the ground before he spread his wings and gained the front of Ru's robe, clinging before climbing his way back up to Ru's shoulder. He cursed all the way up, but Chih didn't care in the least because they recognized that voice.

"Almost Brilliant!"

"Oh, my cleric!"

Another flurry of feathers brought Almost Brilliant over practically into Chih's face, buffeting them about the cheeks with her striped wings before landing on their shoulder.

Chih had thought that Cleverness Himself was a familiar weight on their shoulder earlier, but now they could see that as heavy as he was and as tall, it was nothing like having Almost Brilliant there.

Where she should be, a tiny voice whispered, and Chih put it aside to preen Almost Brilliant's crest.

"Look at you!" Almost Brilliant exclaimed. "Look at how long your hair is, and how thin you have become! Oh what have you been doing in the world without me!"

"Nothing good," Chih said, resisting the urge to grab up Almost Brilliant and hold her to their chest.

"Of course not! Goodness, you should not be allowed out, and if I have my way you won't be until—"

Ru cleared their throat, and Almost Brilliant uttered an irritated trill, a little like the whistle of a kettle.

"I see you as well, acting Divine. Believe me, no one has forgotten you two giants over there. It has been years since I have seen my cleric, and you must wait."

"Bossy woman," Cleverness Himself muttered.

"I need to speak with Myriad Virtues," Ru said, more diplomatically than Chih had expected. "If you could continue the reunion a little distance away?"

Almost Brilliant gave Chih a final peck on their ear and winged her way back to the lion's mouth, snuggling up to Myriad Virtues protectively.

"You may speak to her with friendly eyes on you, acting Divine, or not at all," she said fiercely, and Ru nodded.

"Myriad Virtues, why have you done this?"

"For sorrow," she said. "For grief, and for remembrance. Humans don't understand grief, not like a neixin does."

"It is true, they don't," Cleverness Himself said. "Take away a neixin's grief, and why, perhaps you might have a man."

Ru looked impatient at that, but Chih spoke before they could.

"I don't believe I was ever told about this kind of sorrow," they said. "And if I have been, I am afraid I have forgotten it. Would you please help us to understand?"

"Old-fashioned foolishness," Cleverness Himself cried, and Almost Brilliant might have actually flown straight at him, but Myriad Virtues was already speaking.

"Of course it is old-fashioned. When Cleric Thien and I were new, young men and young women wore flowers in their hair to go courting along the banks of the Hu River, yellow waspmouth and white peony and branches of vermilion catchall like sprays of heart's blood. Now only old women wear them. Soon enough no one will anymore, and the banks of the Hu River will be green and gray and cold."

"It goes back to the Ku Dynasty," Cleverness Himself said abruptly. "In the Ku Dynasty, our wings were clipped when our clerics died, as a symbol of respect and mourning."

There was something strange in his voice, something

about the silence that followed that made Chih's stomach lurch. Those pauses were terrible ones anywhere, but to have it here, in their home and Almost Brilliant's, was brutal.

"Whose respect and whose mourning?" Ru asked, their voice thin.

"Oh, whose do you think?" broke in Almost Brilliant, positively bristling. "Can our claws hold steel shears? Do we love anyone more than we love the sky?"

Chih uttered a soft pained sound, and Cleverness Himself whistled, a noise somewhere between angry and sorrowful. Almost Brilliant tossed her head.

"It is only history," she said. "If we cannot speak of it, then what under the sky is the point of us?"

"It is my history," Myriad Virtues said, her voice stronger than it had been before and now a match for Almost Brilliant's in sharpness. Chih remembered that she was Almost Brilliant's great-aunt.

"It is my history, and it is my grief as well. I do not expect you, clerics, or you, children, to understand. I expect that you cannot, as young as you are. See what happens in twenty years or in forty. See what you do when your time comes."

She suddenly pushed Almost Brilliant out of the nest, making her squawk with dismay before she caught herself and swooped up to Chih's shoulder.

"You must leave me now," she said with great dignity. "I would like to sleep and dream of Cleric Thien."

She retreated to the darkest shadows of the lion's mouth, and after a moment, Chih and Ru made their way to the open part of the aviary.

"She's crazy," Cleverness Himself said, shaking out his feathers. "And that kind of crazy, it's *contagious*."

"She's grief-stricken," Almost Brilliant said wearily. "And if you think you can stop grief by ordering it, Cleverness Himself, you may as well go defend a flock of chickens in Wen, for all the good you are."

She turned her head to nuzzle the side of Chih's face.

"What a wonder it is to see you again," she said softly. "I will give you a proper welcome tomorrow, all right? You can meet the child then."

"I would like nothing better. I'll come at dawn."

Almost Brilliant winged her way back into the aviary, and Cleverness Himself followed after her. It looked like they might be continuing their fight, and Chih was glad to be out of it. Aviary politics were no joke.

Chih and Ru were silent until they gained the entrance, where the lay sister was spinning out some yarn on her drop spindle.

"What on earth was that all about? Is everything all right?" she asked.

Ru frowned, but before they could speak, Chih did.

"Not really. Apparently my old friend who used to steal fish is the acting Divine."

That won a smile from Ru.

"I'll walk you back to the temporary dorms. I'll tell you all about it."

Despite that, they walked in silence. The cicadas had started up again, muted by the stone walls, as relentless as a hundred-year flood or a royal mammoth set against a timber door.

"Ru. What's going on?" Chih asked when they got to the hallway leading to the dormitories.

"The women with the mammoths. They showed up a few days ago. They say that Cleric Thien is their grand-father, and that they will have their body back for proper burial."

"No!"

The word was out of Chih's mouth before they could call it back, hard as a river stone, sharp as flint. Their hands had instinctively balled up into fists as if there was something to fight, and suddenly they very much wanted to fight something. Their anger shocked them, and they forced their hands to relax, their shoulders down from their ears.

"No, of course they can't," Chih said more calmly. "Cleric Thien is not their grandfather, not legally. They have not been for more than forty years. They have no rights here, either under the law of the empress or the northern confederation."

"No, and I'm sure they know that. Tui In Hao, she's an advocate for the Anh courts, so she knows better than most. They are simply convinced that a show of force will sway us."

"Won't it?" Chih asked, and Ru shot them a grimly amused look.

"Will I dishonor Cleric Thien's memory, their chosen life and their work, and allow them to be buried under a name that is no longer their own? Is that what you are asking me?"

Chih blew out an exasperated breath, reaching up to take Ru's smooth face in their hands, making Ru meet their eyes.

"I don't have a neixin's memory, but I still have mine. I know you, and you wouldn't if you had a choice. I'm just saying, are you ready to not have a choice?"

Ru pulled back, their eyes black in the candlelight.

"Singing Hills has always been ready to defend what's ours. We're not going to back down for a pair of mammoths and one foolish advocate."

Eight mammoths, and a count of sixty, Chih didn't say, though they wondered if they should.

"All right," they said instead. "How did you get the post of acting Divine, anyway? Were there no likely looking boulders that wanted the job?"

Ru nudged Chih with a grin. It made them look more familiar, more like the novice who had given Chih their stolen fish when Chih cried in sorrow over rice and rice and rice again.

"The Divine says people change, remember? No one

is as they were five years ago, or two years ago, or a week ago, or a moment ago. If you love someone, you must let them change. And, you know, everyone else wanted to go to Snakehead Lake."

"Ah, of course."

They both hesitated at the entrance to the dorms. When Chih went to hand Ru the candle, they shook their head.

"Take it up and read a while like you're not supposed to. I know my way to bed."

Of course Ru did, but Chih couldn't bear to turn away until Ru disappeared into the darkness, and then even the soft shush of their step and tap of their cane was lost to silence.

Chapter Five

That night, Chih dreamed of an old woman at a barber shop, sitting with her rattan purse in her lap, plucking honey-roasted locusts from a bag and popping them into her mouth. She watched as the barber gave a cleric a smooth shave and threaded the eyebrows of a frowning merchant, and then when he called her to the chair, she held out her hands, her fingers all outstretched.

"You must use the sharpest shears you have," she said sternly. "I want the job done properly."

Chih gasped as they awoke, their heart beating hard and tears in their eyes. They laid their hand over their bare chest, slowing their breath. Before they could quite get it back, there was a whir of feathers and then a hoopoe appeared in the tiny window, poking her sharp face under the reed blind.

"Almost Brilliant!"

Almost Brilliant came in to perch on the edge of the washbasin, tilting her head this way and that.

"What's that?" she asked, and Chih glanced down at the small silver ring threaded through their nipple.

"I got it done in Borsoon. This mammoth scout was

getting his done, and when I came along to see, then they offered to do mine too. It's a little crooked, but I think it's nice."

"Flashy," Almost Brilliant pronounced, "but oh, I am glad to see you. I have been telling my little daughter all about our adventures, and she is so eager to meet you."

"I'm eager to meet her as well. Let me wash and dress, and I'll come along."

"She can wait until after you've had your breakfast. I can see your ribs, and we must fatten you up quickly before you take it in that fluffy head to leave again."

Something in Chih's heart twinged at that, at the idea of leaving without Almost Brilliant by their side, or worse, with some other neixin entirely. It made them want to cry a little, but instead they got dressed and washed, heading down to the kitchens to secure a bowl of salted rice with mustard greens. There was more comfort than they thought there would be in the flavor of a copper pot older than they were, and they were steadier afterwards, as if sadness could be soaked up by cooked rice and wilted greens.

Tye, who had worked in the kitchen since Chih was a toddler, never said much, but he spooned them out a salted plum from the jar he kept in the pantry, a special treat that made Chih smile. They knew better than to thank him, because he did not care to be thanked, but they offered him a little wave with their fingers as they went by, receiving a statesman's grave nod in return.

The aviary was subdued that morning, and as they walked through with Almost Brilliant on their shoulder, they noticed several hoopoes deliberately turning away as they passed.

"We're not popular today," they whispered, but Almost Brilliant only tossed her head.

"I don't need to be popular to be right," she said loudly. "And I am."

She led Chih straight to the back of the aviary, through a tangle of rope and to the rear stone wall. Clerics and laymen did come into the aviary, to clean, to offer up the neixins' fair share of food, once in a great while to mediate where they had been requested, but few came in so far, to where the nesting birds stayed and where the chicks lived until they were big enough to be introduced to the wider world.

Close by the stone wall, Almost Brilliant lifted up from Chih's shoulder, winging her way over to a hollow set some ways above Chih's head. Chih heard a soft conversation, and then a smaller bird exploded from the nest, diving straight for Chih's face.

Oh no, Chih thought, and they turned their head just in time for the fledgling to make contact with their ear in a crashing flurry of feathers and nails.

"Oh, you're Chih, you're Chih!" the young bird called, clinging too hard to Chih's robe and snagging their skin. "Ma has told me so much about you, and look at how *tall* you are and how much *hair* you have! That's too much, isn't it? Ma, is that too much hair? I thought you said that all the clerics were bald like eggs—"

Almost Brilliant followed at a more dignified pace, turfing her daughter off of Chih's shoulder with a grumble. Her daughter squawked, tumbling straight into Chih's surprised hands. Now Chih could see that she was not that much smaller than her mother, though her beak was shorter and her crest was less pronounced. Her coloration was duller as well, and here and there, poking through her smooth feathers, were still several patches of gray fluff, giving her an awkward babyish appearance.

"Introduce yourself properly!" Almost Brilliant scolded from her perch on Chih's shoulder. "Cleric Chih is one of my oldest friends, and you must make a good impression. They are one of the most respected traveling clerics in the order."

That was frankly news to Chih, but Almost Brilliant's daughter gathered herself up with dignity, leaning down to tock her beak twice in deference against Chih's fingers.

"Cleric Chih, I am honored to make your acquaintance. I am called Chiep, descended from the line of Ever Victorious and Always Kind."

"I am so pleased to make your acquaintance as well, Chiep," Chih said. "Your mother is the finest friend anyone could hope for, and I hope for love of her that we will be friends as well."

"We shall be friends for always."

Even with her baby fluff, Chiep looked so solemn at that pronouncement that Chih was struck by her resemblance to the hoopoes painted in the oldest part of the archives, not the bound volumes or even the oldest silk scrolls, but instead painted directly on the walls. They were simple depictions, filled in with smudges of ochre and charcoal and chalk, but Chih had always thought there was such a sense of grace to the drawings, how adoring the painter, and how proud the birds.

Then Chiep rather ruined the effect by hooting loudly, flapping her wings to circle Chih's head in excitement.

"Ma, did you hear? They talked to me! They talked to me, just like you said they would!"

"Am I the first cleric your daughter has met?" Chih asked, startled, and Almost Brilliant whistled, trying to call her daughter back down.

"You are. She properly could have been introduced to someone a few months ago, but you have been gone for some time."

Chih started to ask why Almost Brilliant would wait, but then there was an enormous thump, loud enough to make Chih jerk, followed by a great deal of shouting.

The gate, they thought, and then, *the mammoths.*

Without thinking of it, they ran towards the noise, the hoopoes calling in shock and surprise around them before rising up into the sky.

The gate was still standing when they reached it. They actually weren't sure it would be given the loudness of that crash. The smaller gate was open, and cautiously, Chih approached it, listening to the raised voices from the other side.

"Back that damned animal up!" Ru was shouting. "Get it back from our gates!"

Above them, far above them, Chih couldn't help noticing, was Vi In Yee, sidesaddle on Sho's broad back and looking tense. She whistled, and Sho took two deliberate steps back before reaching up and back to catch something that Vi In Yee threw for her and tuck it into her mouth.

"Of course we will," Tui In Hao said from the ground. "You mustn't be so very frightened, acting Divine. My sister and her mount are both very well trained. They're certainly not going to knock down your gate or your archives unless they're told to do so."

Chih, not directly involved in the conversation, glanced up at where Vi In Yee sat, her mouth tight. Perhaps she did not like her sister's description so much, or perhaps she simply didn't care for the situation as a whole.

"I know how well-trained the southern regiment is," Ru growled. "Now, corporal, kindly prove it by moving your mount back, please."

Another whistle, and Sho pulled back further, already reaching up for another treat. If Tui In Hao was discomforted by that, she gave no sign.

"I do not think that you are foolish, acting Divine. I hope that perhaps you are even reasonable. Therefore see reason. Surrender the body of my grandfather Thien An Lee at once. It is only our right to have our grandfather back, to put him in his proper place by my grandmother's side. You had him for all his long life, and you surely do not need him in death to copy your manuscripts and to talk to your peasants."

Chih moved quickly because they could see Ru's temper welling up, the back of their neck growing red in anger as they pressed the tip of their cane hard into the ground. They came to stand by Ru's side, one hand pressed briefly in warning against the small of Ru's back.

"Cleric Thien was an honored archivist and tutor at Singing Hills," Chih said in their most humble tone. "As many honors as they earned in their secular life, I promise you that they earned just as many here within these halls."

Tui In Hao's lip curled, and she gave Chih a slow and contemptuous blink before responding.

"He wrote to us once or twice, you know. Pages and pages about some dog tribe in the east, their customs, how they carried their babies, probably how they ate string and died bleeding out their mouths and their asses as well. That was what he reckoned his life was worth."

"Oh!" Chih said brightly. "You are speaking about their monograph about the Gao-lai people. They sent that one to the library in Anh. The Head Archivist there actually sent us a commendation for it, and you know they don't do that for just anyone."

Now Tui In Hao looked impatient. She was as tall as Ru, and just as thick through the chest and shoulders, and Chih talked faster.

"It's an impressive award, signed by both the Head Archivist and the Minister of the Left. I wonder, honored advocate, if you would care to come in and see it this evening?"

Tui In Hao opened her mouth, probably to say that she didn't care about who had signed what, but Vi In Yee was faster.

"Sounds fantastic, I want to see that. How about at sunset? We can all sit down to dinner, maybe, unless you're fasting or something?"

Chih almost smiled with relief before they schooled their features back to courtesy. Reasonable. They could both be reasonable, and maybe this wouldn't be so terrible at all.

"You will be very welcome," they said. "And no, we are not fasting, though we are vegetarian. I'm afraid we won't have any meat for you."

"Nah, no problem. We'll bring our own. Anything else we should bring?"

"No, please, do not put yourselves out. We are of course honored by your presence at our table."

Tui In Hao looked between her sister and Chih, and for a moment, Chih thought she might just combust with fury. Then she nodded curtly, giving Ru a hard look.

"This isn't over, acting Divine."

"It isn't," Ru agreed.

Back inside the walls with the small gate closed behind them, Chih let out a shaky breath.

"They're so big up close. I don't know why I keep forgetting, everyone knows that mammoth are big, but— Look at my hands, they're still shaking."

They turned to Ru, but Ru was glaring at them, dark brows lowered over their suddenly very hard eyes. It was such a strange look to see on Ru's face that Chih took a startled step back, their mouth snapping shut.

"Don't do that again," Ru said.

"Ru, she has a mammoth, two of them, and she was furious. We had to get her calmed down, and—"

"No. *I* had to get her calmed down. You have been away for four years, and you have no idea what's going on or what's at stake."

"I think I have a pretty good idea! At least I've *seen* a mammoth before this," Chih snapped. They realized their heart was beating too fast and there was sweat down their back and under their arms despite the chill. They had been more afraid and more angry than they had known.

Ru jerked back as if Chih had slapped them, and then they drew themself up straight, glaring down at Chih from their greater height. It gave Chih a sense of vertigo, how Ru was and wasn't the friend they had known all their life.

"Cleric Chih, you will hold your tongue on things

that do not concern you," Ru said, and Chih had to re-strain the urge to ask them who in the eight hells they thought they were. Instead they folded their hands to-gether neatly in front of them and bowed, just a little too low, just a little too deferential.

"Forgive me, acting Divine. I shall mind myself bet-ter in the future," they bit out, and they didn't rise until Ru snorted and stormed off.

When Ru had gone, Chih straightened, suddenly ex-hausted. They rubbed their hand over their eyes, and Almost Brilliant came to settle on their shoulder.

"Did you see?" they asked, and Almost Brilliant hooted in disapproval.

"Oh, we all saw."

Chih waited for what came next, what they should, could, and didn't do, but instead Almost Brilliant only tugged lightly at their earring.

"Come on," she said. "If they want to see that old com-mendation, we should go dig it out of Cleric Thien's things."

Chapter Six

Cleric Thien had lived in the northern wing of the dormitories for Chih's whole life. At some point, the cleric living next to them had died, and they had quietly taken over the next room as well, filling it from wall to wall with volumes, scrolls, and endless griffonage gathered from the archives. It was all stacked with a kind of desperate tidiness, the floor clear, but when Chih looked closer, they could see a treatise on the gender of honeybees nestled underneath the transcript for a xuanhi opera from the last century. Judging from the rearrangement of some of the volumes, someone had started the task of putting it all in order, but a true accounting was required, and with most of the abbey at Snakehead Lake, it could take a while.

"Cleric Thien's personal library," Chih said, setting down their lamp with a sigh. "That commendation should be in here somewhere."

"It was the plate, the one edged with copper wire. It wasn't that large, so be sure that you look carefully," said Almost Brilliant from her perch on the tallest shelf.

It was tedious work, filthy once they started disturbing

the dust that piled up in the more obscure corners. It was the kind of work that was typically delegated to the younger novices, good practice that also freed up experienced clerics for more difficult tasks.

Chih moved aside a catalog of abortifacient drugs and a study on the mating habits of a rapier finch.

Most of Cleric Thien's collection would be absorbed back into the body of the main archives. Before that, given how thick some of the dust was, there should also be an evaluation as to whether the materials in question were historical, relevant, or truthful. The underground archives were enormous, but they weren't endless, and to earn their place, materials needed to be one or two of those things, ideally all three.

They stacked up a series of seditious pamphlets from the northern confederations, about a magistrate who was truly a fox spirit with a fluffy white tail hidden in her robes and her uncanny handmaiden, an actress with staring white eyes painted over her eyelids.

This could be a decent task for some of the younger novices, perhaps overseen by one of the senior neixin from the aviary. While the neixin did not technically have a voice in what was entered into the proper archives, they certainly had opinions about it, and making a good case for inclusion or exclusion could be—

Chih opened up a trunk that had been holding up several large portfolios of botanical illustrations, and they pulled out a handful of crudely bound books. There was nothing remarkable about them, but when Chih touched the crumbling bark-paper covers, something inside their chest twinged so hard it almost hurt.

Sitting on the dusty floor surrounded by towers of displaced books, Chih opened the first one and read, with some difficulty, *My Days, by Novice Chih,* followed by the date. Apparently, it was a good day since they had gotten some wolfberries on their rice. It was a bad day because Novice Ru was stuck copying lines and couldn't come out to play.

"Look at your handwriting," said Almost Brilliant quietly.

Chih managed a smile.

"Are you going to say it's barely improved?"

"I was actually going to say how neat it was, for all that you were only seven years old."

There were a handful of other volumes from other novices that Cleric Thien had tutored. Chih found Ru's and opened it, finding a drawing of a mammoth on the first page, fortunately labeled, as otherwise they might have thought it was a dog with a long snout. They'd always wanted to see a mammoth, Chih thought with a pang.

In the same trunk, they found the plate that they were looking for, wrapped in a printed saffron cloth, and they got to their feet. They had been bracing themself to go hand it off to Ru, but when they opened the door to the room, they almost ran into a novice in the hallway, the same one who had been watching the door when Chih first returned.

"The acting Divine sent me to find a certain plate," they said proudly, and Chih smiled wryly.

"Sorry, I've beaten you to it," they said, handing it over. "But go ahead, run this back to them."

The novice took it, but before they could run off, Chih stopped them.

"I don't think we've met, have we?"

"No, elder. I am Novice Ngoc."

"Oh, I'm not—" Chih laughed, shaking their head, because actually they were. "I'm pleased to meet you, Novice Ngoc. I'm Cleric Chih. Did you know Cleric Thien?"

"I did, they taught Novice Bi and me about the history of borders and border crossings."

Chih grinned.

"And how to pay a bribe, right?"

At Novice Ngoc's suddenly cagey look, Chih nodded.

"It's all right. Good information is good information."

"Yes, elder," said the novice with relief, and they went on their way with the plate.

For any number of reasons, Chih wanted to be at the dinner that night, but if Ru was playing by the rules, that sort of thing was squarely the province of the Divine, acting or otherwise. If they were requested, they would come, and until they were requested, they had no business with guests of the abbey.

Chih realized that they were actually trying to find a way to skirt the rules and show up anyway, and they shook their head in irritation.

Bad habit, they thought. *They're the acting Divine, no matter how much fish they stole for me.*

Very privately, perhaps they did want Ru to ask for them. It felt wrong to be back at Singing Hills and to know that Ru was doing things without them. That wasn't how things *worked,* and they realized all over again how long they had been gone.

When the summons to dinner didn't come, they instead returned to Cleric Thien's rooms to begin the task of organizing the materials for their return to the main archives. It was tedious but consuming, exactly what they needed at the moment. Almost Brilliant sat with them, and it was almost like old times again, but then she flitted back to the aviary, and they were alone. They didn't realize how much time had passed until they were squinting at the words on the page, and then there was a tap of a cane on the ground behind them and a light knock on the open door.

"Big job," Ru observed.

"Well, I'll get it started anyway. These volumes on the tiger war shouldn't rightly be out of the rare books rooms at all. I can run them back when the archives are open tomorrow. How did it go?"

For a moment, they were worried that Ru would get angry again, but instead they came to sit on the room's single chair, carefully setting their candle in the niche in the wall. Chih saw that their left foot, the bad one, was dragging a little, and they winced.

"That bad, huh?"

"It could have been worse. The corporal doesn't want to knock our doors down or to break our roofs. That's something."

"But I take it Tui In Hao does?"

Ru scowled ferociously, their hand clenching into a fist on their knee.

"Tui In Hao wants a proper burial for the great advocate Thien An Lee," they said bitterly. "She kept going on about the dignitaries that would attend, magistrates and councilmen, merchants from the Five Families, generals in the mammoth corps. She keeps talking about her dead grandmother's standing as a widow in Northern Bell Pass, as if the woman hasn't legally been a widow for longer than we've been alive. It's respect and honor and face, all things that of course we as *simple and unworldly clerics* cannot hope to understand."

"Of course not," Chih said, making a face. "What does Vi In Yee say?"

"That our rice is very good, and she has no idea how we manage to get by without eating meat. Oh, which reminds me."

Ru reached into their robe and pulled out a greasy paper package about the size of two fingers pressed together.

"Here, brought you back something. It's reindeer."

"Ooh."

The fermented reindeer sausage was lean and cut with fattier meat and thin strips of cooked skin, probably pig. It was sour and delicious, and Chih ate the whole thing, licking their fingers.

"I guess I didn't know how hungry I was."

"No idea how you can eat that. I'd be sick for a week."

"You're out of practice."

The silence between them stretched. Chih spread the greasy paper out and folded it into quarters. It could probably be used to start a fire if they dried it out.

"Do you want to be the Divine?" asked Ru, and Chih jumped.

"No! Absolutely not! Why would you ever ask that?"

"Because I do."

"You're *kidding*."

"No. I grew up," Ru said sternly. "I'm thinking about my future and what I want."

"And you want to run all of this." Chih waved, indicating the dorms, aviary, the archives, and the two dozy mammoths outside. By this time of night, Vi In Yee was likely getting them bedded down, making sure they'd eaten enough. War machines needed their sleep.

"I would be good at it," Ru said defiantly. "I've been clerking for the Divine for three years, I'm good at— Tuyet's tits, this is hard to say to you, you know?"

"We said we were going to run off and be pirates, and

you actually stole a boat when Cleric Sun took us down to the docks in Wu."

"Yes, when we were *fourteen*. People grow up. I get to grow up, and I get to change. I'm not going to mope around heartbroken forever because we thought we were both going to get to leave and see the world, and then I couldn't. You can't expect me to be your old friend from home who lives to hear about your great adventures!"

"I never expected that!"

"Then stop thinking that you get to step in and handle things for me!"

"That's not what I'm doing! Tui In Hao was going to bash down the door, and you were practically daring her to do it!"

"She has no right—"

"Of course she doesn't, and that wouldn't have stopped her. Things are different out there, and you should usually be very polite to the woman with the mammoths!"

"You're a cleric of Singing Hills," snapped Ru. "Our authority and our standing is equal to that of the empress's own priests."

"And if the empress's own priests were here, I am certain they would back that up, but right now, they're *not,* and instead, an angry woman with a pair of mammoths at her disposal *is.*"

"I never thought you were a coward."

"I never thought you were an idiot."

They sank into silence. It was full dark now, a scent

of distant rain in the air. Chih had brought no light of their own, and the single candle flame shivered in the draft. Sitting cross-legged on the ground, Chih was close enough to Ru to reach over and touch their knee. They didn't, and they were startled that right now, they didn't even want to.

I should apologize, Chih thought, and then, in their head, someone much younger said *them first.*

It was stupid and childish, and Chih opened their mouth to say sorry when they both heard it.

It was a soft step on the floor, bare feet padding on a thin wool rug that had been brought all the way from the city of Boddo in Akushla. Two steps, followed by a sigh, and if the steps hadn't convinced them, the sigh did, a breath drawn between the teeth and then exhaled in a soft whistle. It was the sigh of a cleric who was perhaps dismayed at their charges, but all right, they would explain again, and Chih's hands flew up to cover their mouth, the fine hairs on the back of their neck trying to stand upright.

The steps shushed across the carpet, from the window, Chih thought, to the bed. Their belly clenched with fear and dread, and over it a kind of desperate hope as well.

Everyone made a mistake. Of course it was a mistake, everyone thought they were dead, but they weren't.

A hand dropped on their shoulder, and they nearly shrieked before they realized it was Ru, bending over in their chair so that their face was close to Chih's. The candlelight hollowed Ru's face, gave it skull-like edges.

"Chih?" they whispered, and Chih shook their head, grabbing for Ru's hand. Ru's fingers were ice-cold; theirs weren't much better.

They listened as the steps crossed from the bed to the small altar on the wall, and it was easy to imagine Cleric Thien there, making their obeisance to Gentleman Bell, their patron, kissing his coin and perhaps anointing it with a tiny droplet of blood from a needle-prick to their finger.

A memory returned to Chih, unbidden, of being so small that they and Ru both fit under Cleric Thien's bed. They remembered squeezing shoulder to shoulder next to Ru, peering out through the drape of the tasseled bedspread, watching Cleric Thien talk to their patron god.

Cleric Thien told Gentleman Bell how they wished for fish for the people on the river and goats for the people on the mountain. They wished for peaceful dreams for all their family, the living and the dead alike. They wished that the Gentleman's mouth would always be filled with blood, so that he would never again feel the urge to devour his men.

"And I wish," they continued in the same voice, "that Novice Chih and Novice Ru know that *I can see them*."

They'd spun around on the ball of their bare foot, lunging at the two children under the bed who shrieked with delight at being chased and caught.

But there was a moment, Chih thought, staring so hard at the cracked door between the two rooms, *where it wasn't delight. It was terror at being caught, and now—*

Another sigh, and then a moan, a soft one as if of an old cleric waking from a troubled sleep, and then there was a loud bang, something hard hitting the floor.

Almost as one, Ru and Chih rose up, Chih by Ru's side as if they had never left, and they both threw themselves towards the cracked door. Chih shoved it open, and Ru lifted their candle high to throw the light as far as they could and they saw—

"Nothing," Chih said, looking around at the cluttered room. The window that they had opened earlier was open still, letting in just a thin sliver of grayish moonlight. It was overcast, a good night for scares, Cleric Thien themself would have said. They had liked ghost stories very much, the true ones about the old soldiers who still lurked on the battlefields and the false ones, made to frighten children and fools away from deep water or tiger tracks, told so long they became a different kind of true.

Ru took a few candle stubs from the box by the door and lit them one by one, placing them on the desk, the nightstand, and the windowsill. In the bright candlelight, Gentleman Bell smiled over a small ceramic bowl stained with more than thirty years of offerings.

"We should ask if Vi In Yee and Tui In Hao want to take him home," Chih said, tearing their eyes away from the niche. "There may be other things here they would like too."

"Yes. I asked them to come to the talking ceremony tomorrow night. We can ask them then."

"You did?"

"It seemed polite. It was a very polite dinner, all told."

The tightness around Ru's mouth suggested that it had stayed polite because everyone felt very close to a fight and no one wanted to be blamed for starting it. That was fine. Chih had seen a lot get done when everyone involved was on the edge of a brawl.

Chih wanted to sit on the bed and talk about what came next, what preparations had to be made, whether the Divine would make it back in time, what food they might send for from the town down the road. That would be easy, even appropriate. Instead they took a deep breath, letting it out slowly.

"Do you think that was them?" they asked in a small voice.

"It was Cleric Thien or something that wanted to be mistaken for them," Ru said, and they both considered that idea: a cleric improperly laid to rest or something terrible actually walking the halls, looking to eat the forgotten and the alone.

"I'll get—What would you say to me grabbing some of the warding bells out of storage? I could hang them up before I went to bed."

Ru shot them a wry look, but they nodded. It would

take some time before they were used to this, either of them, but so far as either of them knew, they had plenty of it. No better time to start than the present.

"Here, I've got the key, if you want it. Mrs. Chao is in charge of storage while Cleric Hahn is gone, and she never comes in until past midday."

Chih took the key wordlessly, biting back a comment about foxes and the inadvisability of letting them into the imperial coffers. This was going to take some getting used to.

Together they put out the candles and closed the windows. The room looked abandoned, for all that Cleric Thien had only been dead for a few weeks. Somehow, the books and blankets and boxes full of strange curiosities knew that something was over, and they grieved in their own inanimate way.

The night air was a relief, and Ru handed Chih the candle.

"Are we all right?" Ru asked, and Chih nodded.

"Of course we are. We've got work to do, don't we?"

"*Work first, worry later,*" Ru said in a decent imitation of Cleric Thien. "Right. Talk to you tomorrow?"

"Wait."

Ru did so, but silently, and Chih felt a pang of loss for their friend who couldn't bear for a room to be silent. They took a deep breath.

"I shouldn't have talked over you. I'm sorry about that."

"Thank you. I'm sorry I shouted at you."

Neither of them could quite look at each other, which was new, but Chih found that it was bearable as well. They were changing, and Cleric Thien had always said that change hurt, but it was bearable if you watched it, if you accepted it and knew that it was always coming.

"And I'm sorry you had to stay home when I left."

Ru looked surprised at that, and then chagrined. They tapped their cane impatiently on the ground.

"It's what happened. Sickness happens. Disability happens. I don't need you to be sorry."

"I'm sorry for myself too," Chih said. "I missed you. Every day. I don't know if I ever told you that."

"I missed you too," Ru said, and deliberately, they stepped in to lean against Chih, shoulder against shoulder like they used to. Ru loomed more than they used to, but it was something that hadn't changed, that pressure, that relief of *oh, it's you, thank goodness.*

They pulled back, and there was still plenty to say, but that was about all they could take for the moment.

"And anyway," said Ru, sounding more like themself, "I finally did get to see a mammoth."

"What'd you think?"

"Big. Impressive. Now I'd like to see a little less of them."

Chih made their way to storage, where they pulled out a box containing a dozen yellow ropes, all hung with sweetly chiming brass bells. The bells were brought out and blessed routinely by clerics from the Order of the Shrike, who knew better than anyone else what to do with the walking dead, and on consideration, Chih took the whole box with them.

They hung a strand around the plane tree where Cleric Thien liked to read, another on their shelf in the archives, where they kept some of the heavier things they couldn't drag back to their rooms. There were plenty of places where Cleric Thien or a spirit pretending to be them might go, but finally, down to the last few ropes, Chih returned to their room. Ropes went over the doorways, and then Chih realized that the window was open again, the shutters parted to let in a breath of fresh air.

"I thought I closed that," Chih said to themself, but they knew there was no *might have* about it.

They closed and locked the window again, and they hung a blessed belled rope over it.

Finally, feeling all the time as though there was someone just beyond sight in the shadows, they hurried to bed.

Chapter Seven

Chih woke the next morning to a juvenile hoopoe hopping on their shoulder. Chiep didn't peck like her mother would, but her claws were sharp and Chih grunted, twitching to get her off.

"I could have sworn I latched that window," they said in a wry echo of the night before.

"The shutters are easy, everyone can open them. But you're awake! Look, you're awake!"

"I am. Good morning, Chiep, is there anything—"

"Mother wants to see you right away. It's important."

"Right. Let me get my clothes on."

As they dressed and splashed some water on their face, Chiep fluttered around the room, exclaiming over everything she saw and would remember, from the picture of the hoopoe on the wall to the untidy pile of Chih's traveling things.

"I am going to remember all of this," Chiep said gleefully, and Chih hid a smile.

"Want a lift?" Chih asked, raising their shoulder slightly, and Chiep was so pleased she was almost silent the whole way to the aviary, only occasionally burbling with excitement.

"Maybe someday I can go with you?" Chiep asked, and then she nearly fell off of Chih's shoulder in a fit of nervous giggles. "I mean, only if you want, and if I do well at my tests and if Ma says it's all right, of course!"

"We could go see the capital together maybe," Chih said with a smile. It would be interesting to be the cleric for Chiep's first venture into the world, when she'd gotten her adult name. At the same time, Chih got a slight pang because that would mean that it wasn't Almost Brilliant accompanying them to the capital, where they'd both eaten spicy roasted grubs for the first time and where they had taken their first trip by sea.

The doorkeeper nodded them into the aviary, which was hung with a strange silence that morning. Even Chiep became more subdued, nestling closer to the side of Chih's neck as she directed them to a nesting box, this one a small wooden tea crate stuffed liberally with straw and scraps of old fabric. A strand of blue trailed from the sawed opening, a scrap of some old cleric's robes.

Chih thought that Chiep would fly into the box, but instead she stayed on Chih's shoulder, hopping a little nervously from left to right.

"Ma! Ma, I've brought the cleric."

Almost Brilliant came out of the nesting box, shooing her daughter off to take her place.

"Good morning, trouble," Chih said, and Almost Brilliant gave them a light peck on the jaw.

"You have no idea. Listen. Listen to me."

"I always do."

"You have to get Myriad Virtues a seat at the ceremony tonight."

For a moment, Chih had no idea what Almost Brilliant was speaking of, and then they remembered.

"Well, of course they'll be there," Chih said, surprised. "I imagine all of the aviary will be there."

"In the rafters, on the windowsills," Almost Brilliant said impatiently. "In our official capacity as recorders. Myriad Virtues needs a seat, she must be allowed to speak, do you understand me?"

"If anyone deserves it, it's her. But I've never seen—Ow!"

This time the peck was harder and far less affectionate. Chih had to stop themself from instinctively reaching up to swat Almost Brilliant away. She had come close to drawing blood.

"I do not care!" Almost Brilliant said fiercely. "She wants a seat, and she will speak."

"And the rest of the aviary?"

Almost Brilliant whistled, sharp enough that the sound drilled into Chih's ear.

"You are not talking to the rest of the aviary, you are talking to me, Myriad Virtues' grand-niece."

Chih was abruptly aware of eyes on them, the other

67

neixin watching from their perches, tilting their heads from one side to another. There was something alien about them suddenly, for all that Chih had grown up with neixin everywhere. They were people, but they weren't human, the Divine had always said, and right now, the difference between bird and human was very stark.

"I think I would like to speak to Myriad Virtues," Chih said slowly, and Cleverness Himself hooted derisively from his perch.

"Oh, would you? Fancy that. So would I."

Almost Brilliant had been all but trembling on Chih's shoulder, and at Cleverness Himself's words, she threw herself at him, sending him into flight. It wasn't a serious brawl, not one that would send blood drops raining down and leave one party or the other quite plucked, but Chih wouldn't want to be the target of such a flight, and apparently, Cleverness Himself didn't either. He settled down next to Chiep, who was watching things from the top of the nesting box, and Almost Brilliant left off to return to Chih's shoulder.

"She will not speak to us," Almost Brilliant said tersely. "She asked for a place at the ceremony, and she has not spoken since."

"And what good's a neixin that won't talk?" Cleverness Himself snorted.

"Why won't she speak?" asked Chih, too shocked to wait for more. They had never heard of a neixin that couldn't speak. Their ability to speak wasn't connected

to vocal cords that could never manage a human regis-
ter, but instead to what they were, something ancient
and tied to the order of Singing Hills itself.

"She refuses," said Cleverness Himself, and Almost
Brilliant trilled angrily.

"She refuses to speak to *you*. But she deserves her
place. She must have it. Cleric. Chih."

Being fixed with Almost Brilliant's diamond-hard gaze
was almost painful. Worse than the anger was the grief
there, something that would shriek and claw for whatever
might relieve it, even for an hour, even for a moment.

"I'll talk to Ru," they said.

They looked over to the lion's mouth, where Myriad
Virtues sat stiller than still, little more than a ball of
lusterless feathers. Chih realized that she had stopped
preening herself. If she heard their talk, she gave no
sign. She did not speak at all, and Chih left the aviary in
the echoing, grieving silence.

Chih went to find Ru directly, but the issue was that Ru
wasn't there to be found. They had left before dawn to lay
in supplies for the evening, and, frustrated, Chih ended
up back in Cleric Thien's quarters to organize things until Ru returned.

By day, the room lost all of its dread. The belled ropes
looked ostentatiously paranoid, but Chih left them up as
they opened the windows again. The cool breeze coming

in set the bells ringing from time to time, a sweet and melancholy counterpoint to the dismantling of a life.

The piles rose up around them, things to be returned, things to be sorted, things to be disposed of. There was so much, and more than once, Chih had to go to the window and the fresh air before they could properly breathe again. Mostly they were able to separate the task from why they were doing it. They could sort books, fold clothes, arrange things in order by date. It was only work, and they could always work.

From time to time, people appeared at the door, the few clerics remaining, the lay brothers and sisters, even Novice Ngoc and their friend Novice Bi. The people hovered, unsure of what to say, but determined to say it. Their sympathy was a weight like heavy wool on Chih's shoulders, and they found themself a guardian of the sympathy and the kind wishes, not always a comfortable place to be when their own grief lurked.

Chih looked up when the light started to go, realizing abruptly that they were starving. They had missed breakfast to go to the aviary, and thinking about Myriad Virtues and her grief made them tear up. They dashed the tears away in annoyance.

By then Ru was back, and Chih went to help them unload the ox, bringing the food, the incense, and the beeswax candles into the remembrance hall. Cleric Thien's remains had been shielded from the room by a wooden screen, and someone had already put down the cushions and the low tray tables for the evening to come.

"The Divine will not be here tonight," Ru said. "I heard in town. A rockslide took out a good chunk of the road. They'll have to go around. They might be a few days yet."

"They'll be sorry to miss this," Chih mused, setting down the bottles of rice wine. "But Ru. I've been in the aviary. Myriad Virtues is grieving."

"She and Cleric Thien were close. She never went traveling again after they broke their ankle that last time and decided to stay at the abbey permanently."

"Almost Brilliant asked if she could be given a place. Not on the windowsills or the rafters, but with us."

The moment Chih said it, they knew it had come out wrong. Almost Brilliant wasn't asking, and this made her sound like a supplicant. Before they could correct themself, however, Ru was already looking around.

"Where would we put a neixin? All of the spaces are taken up. Tui In Hao is bringing her entire entourage. Wouldn't she be better off with the other neixin anyway?"

Chih scowled at that, but then Ru was pulled away by one of the lay sisters, something about the food for the night. They trailed along impatiently, but it was one thing after another, and then it was time to go get ready, to pull out the formal indigo robes that they hadn't worn in years, to take out their earrings, and to finally get their head shaved. Of course Cleric Binh, who usually looked after such matters, was away at Snakehead Lake, and the lay brother who they finally found to do it was clumsy with the razor, nicking the back of their scalp rather badly.

Chih was just cleaning out the cut with willow water when Almost Brilliant whistled from the window.

"If you kept yourself properly shaved, this wouldn't happen to you so much."

"I know. Almost Brilliant—"

"You will have to bring her to the hall," Almost Brilliant said sternly. "She cannot fly."

Chih had forgotten somehow, and after cleaning up the thread of blood that ran down the back of their neck, they went to the aviary again, Almost Brilliant tense on their shoulder.

"Hello, Myriad Virtues," Chih murmured. "Are you well tonight?"

The neixin looked at Chih with eyes that were calm and bright, but she did not respond. For a moment, they thought she might open her mouth to reveal a tongue that was cut away as surely as her primary feathers, but of course that was foolish, and Chih took a deep breath.

"It is time for Cleric Thien's talking ceremony. Will you come?"

Chih held their hand to the lion's mouth, and after a moment, Myriad Virtues climbed on, her motions slow and laborious. She felt oddly heavy as Chih brought her to their chest, limp and inert like a bundle of rags.

By their ear, Almost Brilliant whistled softly with relief.

"All right, have you got her? Let's go." And then belatedly, "You do look very nice. Every bit a proper cleric. Cleric Thien would be proud."

When they reached the remembrance hall, it buzzed with activity, people coming in and out, laying out the delicate meals with their beakers of rice wine on the trays before each cushion. Chih recognized the novice from the night before, Ngoc, trimming and lighting the candles while another novice, taller and more considered in their motions, tidied their placement in Ngoc's wake. The seats were arranged in two rows facing the central walkway. At the head of the hall, in the place of honor, lay Cleric Thien. Ru's place as acting Divine was beside it, and Chih almost yelped with surprise when Ru bumped their shoulder, passing from behind.

"Sit up at the front, next to me. This is going to be an interesting night."

"Ru, I need to talk to you about Myriad Virtues—"

Chih tried to grab their sleeve, but they were gone again, off to attend to something Cleric Yu-Ching needed. Almost Brilliant hissed with frustration.

"I'll peck their head in," Almost Brilliant swore. "I'll haunt them with every time they pissed themselves as a child."

"Please don't," Chih said, but then the doors opened and the northern contingent appeared.

Gasps echoed through the hall, and even Chih, who had spent nearly a year in the northern confederation, was startled.

Tui In Hao was dressed for mourning in sheerest silk, six layers or more, all in varying shades of cream and ivory. Cut to different lengths, they swirled around her legs as she walked, giving her all the menace of a blizzard on the move. Her black hair was oiled so that it shone, and her long braids draped over her shoulder, carved bone beads hanging from the tassels and clicking gently as she moved.

Behind her was her sister, taller and in the dress uniform of the mammoth corps. Unlike Tui In Hao's traditional white, Vi In Yee's uniform consisted of a long burgundy tunic split up the sides over wide trousers tucked into soft boots. A silver-tipped goad hung from her belt, and she had painted two crescent moons at her temples, the horns circling her eyes. She looked uneasy in the remembrance hall, her quick dark gaze scanning the walls and the high windows as if to see where she might make her escape.

Their entourage consisted of perhaps a half dozen men and women, mostly dressed as Vi In Yee was with one or two minor adjuncts in tow. Chih noted with faint unease how odd the military uniforms looked at Singing Hills. They knew the value of a uniform, of an identity that could be signified at a glance. The indigo robes of a cleric helped them secure aid and eased situations that required calm and comfort. The uniform of the mammoth corps of the north, empire breakers and law keepers, stood for something else.

Before Chih could worry too much, a slight quarrel broke out, who sat where and with whom, and they stepped in to aid the lay sister and Ru to get things settled. There were seats for everyone, and then Ru was taking the officiant's place at the head of the hall, nodding for Chih to join them.

In their hands, Myriad Virtues trembled, and Chih looked around desperately only to find every seat filled. Several solutions flashed through their head as the room quieted and heads turned to see the delay. Chih's cheeks grew red, and they headed to the front of the hall, trying not to duck their head and scurry.

A cleric always knows who they answer to, Cleric Thien whispered in their head. *They heed the Divine of their order, and after that, they heed their gods.*

Chih kept their back straight, and when they came to the seat Ru had indicated, instead of sitting down, they gently lowered Myriad Virtues to the table, beside the dish of steamed barley and the plate of roasted, salted root vegetables that had been Cleric Thien's favorite.

Myriad Virtues twisted her head back and forth to see the people seated around her, and then with utmost gentleness, she preened the side of Chih's finger, a thank-you that made Chih's heart ache with guilt at not having done more.

They caught Ru's eyes as they stood up, a look of confusion and irritation. Chih shrugged very slightly as they walked past: *Well, you could have listened when I asked.* They made their way to kneel with the lay brothers and sisters, the ones who would not speak during the ceremony. They knew what they were giving up. They were sorry, but they also knew that they were right.

Tui In Hao had no such assurances, and she glowered from her seat, rapping the hilt of her sword on the ground to produce a sharp, explosive sound.

"What is this?" she asked, her voice cold. "We were told that this was a funeral, not a flying circus."

In the rafters above, the neixin had come to take their place, and at Tui In Hao's words, there was a rustle of feathers and a few angry calls. Ru glanced up sharply, a gesture that Chih knew they'd copied from the Divine, and the neixin settled. Ru nodded, and then they turned a hard eye to Tui In Hao.

"This is a funeral," they said, their voice almost placid. "The people who are seated tonight have memories to share about Cleric Thien. The neixin, the jewels of Singing Hills, listen and remember. Nothing spoken here will be forgotten. We have allowed you and your people a space here, advocate."

Chih could tell that Tui In Hao had caught the *allowed*, but before she could open her mouth to take issue with it, Vi In Yee spoke up.

"No one told us that Grandfather's bird could tell stories," she said. "Ought to be good."

To Chih's relief, Tui In Hao only narrowed her eyes and nodded once.

"I hope it is," she said frostily, laying her sword next to her on the ground.

"We always hope to live up to your expectations for us," Ru said. It was sharper than the Divine would have said it, without that bland peacefulness that had left kings and warlords wondering if they had been insulted, but it wasn't bad, Chih reckoned, and Ru continued smoothly.

"Thank you, clerics of Singing Hills, advocate Tui In Hao, Corporal Vi In Yee, mammoth corps riders, and lay disciples. We come together tonight to eat food that nourished Cleric Thien in life, to say farewell, and to celebrate their departure into what follows, which we cannot know, though we at Singing Hills have a few stories about it."

The last was uttered with a slight smile, and Chih knew why. It was what Cleric Thien had told the youngest novices when they were anxious about the world and what came after it.

Chih wished they could meet Ru's eyes to show them they understood, but they were in the shadows, and as the lay disciples walked around to light the candle stubs at every tray table, the night took her place and the ceremony began.

Chapter Eight

Ru took a sip of their rice wine, smiled, and looked up. In that moment, they were and weren't the cleric Chih had grown up with. This was someone new, and something in Chih ached, because growing up, growing older, was always a kind of loss, even if what was gained repaid it all and then some.

When they spoke, the tenderness in their voice had a wry twist to it, their smile a little crooked.

When I first came to Singing Hills, I was six years old. I cried all the time. I missed my parents and my sheep and my dog. The clerics at Singing Hills could tell me all they liked that these things were gone, but I didn't believe them, not for an instant, because more real than their story of a sickness that struck at the lungs and the throat was the fact that my ma had told me that wherever I was, I could always follow the river home.

I had already made a few tries for the river. Usually someone brought me back in an hour or two and tried to explain to me that home wasn't there anymore, that

Singing Hills was now my home, and that they loved me and wanted what was best for me. They were right, but I was six, and no less stubborn than I am today.

I figured that the problem was that I had run off without a plan. This time, I didn't tell anyone, not even my new best friend Chih. I would get home, and my ma would clear up the misunderstanding. Maybe they would send Chih to sleep over, and that would be good. But first I had to get home.

I thought I was being so smart. I found some clothes that sort of fit me from the donation boxes, and I stashed a bag of food under the bed. I woke up when it was still dark, and I went down to the water that I knew would take me home.

Everything was going so well, and then I came around the first bend and found Cleric Thien sitting on a log as if they were waiting for me, Myriad Virtues on their shoulder and a walking stick by their side. I stopped, ready to run if they tried to catch me or tell me it was time to go back to the abbey, but instead they only reached into their bag.

"Here," they said. "I'll bet you haven't eaten yet."

I hadn't, and they pulled out a green onion bun, my favorite. I sat next to them on the log, and they ate one as well, saying nothing. When we were done, they stood up and offered me their hand.

"Well, come on," Cleric Thien said. "We have a bit of a walk ahead of us, don't we?"

They let me lead the way, and we walked for three days, following the bend of the river. It's a long way to travel, made even longer by a six-year-old who needs constant minding not to fall into the water or rush headlong into danger. The closer we got, the more familiar the trees looked, the faster I wanted to go. I was almost home, and my heart wanted to burst for all the things that it couldn't hold.

I told Cleric Thien that my ma would be so happy to see us, and that my father would take us out back to meet my sheep. They could meet my dog, Banh, who was tan all over except for a little sprinkle of white sugar over her shoulders. She could do tricks. There was a tree behind the house that walked at night sometimes, and you could tell because some mornings, it was in a slightly different place than it had been when we'd gone to sleep.

I told Cleric Thien and Myriad Virtues all about it, and they nodded and asked me questions and said how very good it all sounded, how kind my parents were and how cute my dog.

Of course there is only one way for this story to end.

We came around the final bend of the river, and instead of the noise of a village by the water, there was nothing. There was only a silence that seemed all the greater for the clack of reed wind chimes hanging from the eaves. Everyone in the village had them, you know, cut to different lengths, notched to let the wind blow through them. In a storm, their music rang to the opposite bank and back, calling in anyone who was outside.

I remember Cleric Thien took my hand. They were silent, and they followed along as I ran home, looking for the things and the people that made it home, and of course, they weren't there, and they never would be again.

I fell down into my old bed, which was wet and cold from the hole in the roof, and I cried for what felt like hours. When I woke up, Cleric Thien was building a fire in the hearth, and Myriad Virtues was on the windowsill, looking around. When they had gotten a soup going, they reached up to take something from the shelf over my bed. I saw it was a stone carving of a wild pig, smooth from how often I had held it in my hands, as familiar as my own face.

"Here," Cleric Thien said. "Will you tell me about this?"

I came to sit next to them and as the soup boiled, I told them about the little stone pig. I told them about how my paternal uncle had brought it back from the riverlands when he went out there to trade, and how it was supposed to channel the strength of a great warrior who was raised by wild pigs, a man called Wild Pig Yi. I told him about how when I had a fever last year, my ma had let me hold it in bed, pressing the stone against my cheek to keep me cool.

I told them all that, and then when I gave it to them to hold, they told me about it too, how long it was and how heavy. It was made of a kind of speckled marble that we don't have here in the west, and they turned it over to show me the maker's mark cut into one tiny hoof, the character for rosemary and sweetness at once. If I could find the maker, they said, I might find the pig's siblings, a whole stone family discovered if I only knew to look and see.

At the end, Cleric Thien sighed.

"You know, rightfully, we should leave this here. That's a good lesson, isn't it? At Singing Hills, we deal in memory. The things we remember last as long as we do and longer. The thing itself, well, it goes away. It breaks. It sinks to the bottom of the river. It dies or leaves or is lost."

Then they handed it to me, telling me to put it in my bag and keep it very well, because it was precious.

"Come on," they said. "We'll eat, and then you can tell me and Myriad Virtues all about your mother and your father and your sheep and Banh."

I still have that stone pig in my room, and it is very precious to me. It was a lesson in the purpose that Singing Hills serves, and how memory is greater than death. It was also love and compassion, passed from a cleric who is gone to the one who lives on after, and it should never be forgotten.

Someone in the room sighed, and Chih let out a careful breath. They had known the story before, and now the archives knew it as well, a small piece of kindness that would last so long as Singing Hills did.

Ru drained their rice wine and blew out their candle. From their place on the sidelines, Chih thought they looked tired but pleased. It was a good story.

"Advocate Tui In Hao. Will you speak?"

Tui In Hao frowned, wary as if Ru had set her some trap, but she nodded. For several long moments she gazed into the candle flame flickering in front of her, and when she spoke, her voice was calm and measured, smooth and as strong as silk.

I have been an advocate employed by the empire since I was seventeen. I passed the regional examinations, and then the national ones, and while most of my work keeps me on the coast and in the capital, during the first years of my practice, I was stationed at the posthouse at Ko-anam Ford.

It's a desolate post, especially in winter. On the border between the north and the south, the nights cast long shadows, and sometimes, the only thing you can do to drive back the things that live in darkness is to tell stories.

One long night, I joined the guards who watch the border, waiting for trouble on either side. They gave me barley wine to drink, and one of them, an old woman with one arm, asked me if I knew that my grandfather, the famous Thien An Lee, had tried a case at the very posthouse where I was stationed.

It was long ago, and likely no other advocate had cared to come all the way out to the border to represent a young man accused of poaching.

The young man in question had killed a stag. That is not such a serious thing on the border, not like it would be in a royal preserve. Almost everyone in the north does some poaching, though mostly they take rabbits and quail. Still the winter was long, and the young man had a family to feed. He thought one larger crime might serve better than several smaller ones.

My grandfather was confused and irritated to be brought halfway to Ingrusk to try such a ridiculous thing. The tribunal was demanding the young man's hands and his tongue, a severe punishment that required oversight from the capital.

My grandfather almost accepted the ruling the hour he arrived, but then he decided to look further into the matter. He spoke with the young man, who was frozen with fear, and he learned some interesting things.

He learned that when the young man had shot the deer, it had turned into a woman, and not just any woman, but the grandmother from a notable local clan. What a great shame it is, to find out that a grandmother of such a noble clan has been changing her skin, and to be forced to recover her naked body, bloodied and covered with deer fat, from the forest. Shapechanging is an unclean kind of magic in that region, associated with the families who tend to the dead and who appease the night spirits.

He also learned that two members of the tribunal that demanded the young man's mutilation, a sentence designed to keep him from speaking or writing of what he had seen, were members of that selfsame clan, and he grew thoughtful.

At the young man's defense, he showed up to the chamber as a dandy from the capital, his judicial robes trimmed with peacock feathers and wearing his spectacles of smoked glass. He came straight up to the bench to tell them what a fine time he had been having, how generous his hosts were, as if he was at a new year's banquet and not a trial. He produced wine he had brought all the way from home, pouring them each a measure and taking one for himself as well, and only then was he ready to start.

"Honored justices of Ko-anam. I will keep my argument short, because the nights here are long, and they are better suited to drinking the health of the moon, reading poetry, and praising beautiful women. As advocate for this young man, I see that you have asked for the most severe penalty possible for the crime of poaching a deer, a penalty so severe, I would say, it was more suitable for the death of a woman, perhaps an old woman of a venerable clan. What a strange thing, I thought. Surely some mistake has been made. Instead, I ask that you simply allow this young man, who has never stood in front of this tribunal before, who has upon his shoulders the weight of a household and a family name, to depart only responsible for the standard fine of poaching a deer. If he cannot pay it, let him go into indenture for a year, and if he can, then the county is well compensated for the loss."

Here he paused, taking a sip from a tiny flask hung around his neck before going to stand contemplatively before the fire.

"It is difficult, what one doesn't know, isn't it?" he asked, almost to himself. "They keep us advocates in training for seven years, cramming precedent into our brains until we go to sing our baby siblings a song, and all that comes out are the laws regulating the width of roads and the trees that may be planted alongside. When I passed the examinations and took my place, I did not know my new nephew's name, much to my sorrow. It is a shame that a young man did not know the full consequences of killing the deer. He thought it was only a single animal that might feed his family, nothing more. If he had known otherwise, he would have acted differently, I am sure."

One of the members of the tribunal began to speak, but my grandfather continued, still gazing at the flames.

"And of course one can drink poison without thinking of it. Why, in the capital, it is so common a thing to poison one's enemies that it is the fashion to wear the antidote around one's throat, so one is not unfortunately caught out at parties."

The tribunal members rose from their seats, calling for the guard, but my grandfather took the vial from around his neck and held it over the flames.

"It can change your life, what you don't know," he said very mildly. "And sometimes, if one is forgiven, it does not need to change anything, does it?"

They let the young man go, the fine heavy but not more than he could bear, and my grandfather shared with all the members of the tribunal a little of the peppery ginger juice he liked to keep in the vial he wore, because it kept his breath fresh and aided in his digestion.

They never knew that they had been tricked, and my grandfather had a word with the young poacher as well, because the things you knew could be as dangerous as the things you didn't, and the man moved his family south and far away from what he knew.

And then my grandfather returned home to his wife and his life, and he lived there peacefully and happily until of course he didn't.

Tui In Hao drained her cup and put out her candle, staring around almost defiantly to see if anyone would question her story. Above them, in the rafters, the neixin chirped softly among themselves, and Chih knew they were asking after the particulars, who the members of the tribunal were, what did it mean to be a grandmother and a shapechanger, what had become of the poacher and his family. They doubted they would get those answers— Tui In Hao had left them out deliberately, and it would have to serve as it stood.

"Thank you for your story, advocate," Ru said, and Chih could tell that they meant it. It was another face to Cleric Thien that neither of them had ever guessed at, clever and a little ruthless.

There were a few surprises like that from the stories that came afterwards, both from the northern entourage and the clerics of Singing Hills. They felt like pieces of wood coming together to build a bridge, and at the far side, there was Cleric Thien, born Thien An Lee.

There were stories that Chih could have told, wanted to tell, but they found they were not particularly hurt by the missed chance. They could read their stories into the archives later if they wished, or they could hold them close for a while. There was no urgency. Instead they knelt and listened, and at the same time, they watched Vi In Yee with an increasingly worried eye.

She wasn't a woman who did well with idleness, that was clear, and she had brought her own alcohol in with her, carried in a hollow bone flask sealed with wax. She broke the seal not long after Tui In Hao's story, and she had been drinking steadily for a while now, slouching first a little and then a lot, turning her head more slowly with each speaker who snuffed out their candle.

Finally, the hall was nearly dark, and she raised her head to speak.

These are good stories. They're all good stories. They're sad stories, too. Makes me want to cry into my soup, what a waste. And I have stories about Granddad, I do. I never met him, though, and neither did you, Tui-ah. He was gone before we were born.

Instead he was just like . . . Like this story, you know? This story that sat at the head of the table and would expect us to be perfect, no matter who we were and what we did. He didn't even have to be there to make us behave, not when—

Tui-ah, do you remember how we'd go to the lake? You know, the house on Blind Horse Lake. And you remember. You remember how there were one hundred steps exactly to get from the beach to the house, right? We'd count them as we ran up and down, all summer.

And you remember. Grandma couldn't go with us. She died two months ago. She was a good lady. She raised us after our parents got divorced, loved us a lot. She was great. Sad a lot. Lonely a lot. She died. Liver thing. I mean, we all knew it was coming, got to say goodbye and all. Last thing she told me was that I needed to get married. I mean, what do I need to get married for? I have two mammoths.

Anyway, Grandma couldn't go with us because her

leg was so bad she couldn't get up and down the hundred stairs at the lake house.

And that was. That was *sad*. Because we loved her, right? We didn't think about it because we were kids. Our whole lives, Grandma can't come to the lake house with us because her leg's too weak and it makes her cry when she's on it too long.

So I'm a kid, and I think she's always been this way, that she's always been old, and she could never go to the lake house, but I'm wrong, because she told me one year when we were packing to go that I should look for tern eggs on the west side of the island, down the ravine that leads to the water. She said they tasted good if you bored a hole in the small end with your knife and sucked out the yolk.

I asked her how she knew that, and she said that it was her father's house, wasn't it? She had grown up there, and after she was married, she had gone every year until Granddad broke her leg.

I couldn't believe it. Break her leg? He broke her leg, and I don't know why she told me. Maybe it was the day, or maybe it was just because she was tired of no one knowing. Maybe she liked me best and it was fine, or she liked me least, and it was fine.

She said they had fought, less than a year after they married. It was about money. Something about money, something like he was spending it where he shouldn't have been, her numbers weren't adding up.

He turned away from her, and she followed after him, demanding answers that he didn't want to give. This was at the house in Northern Bell Pass, you know. She was telling me this just a few rooms over from where it happened. I know how steep those stairs are there.

I asked her, *Did he push you?*

She didn't say anything. She told me to get packed and to remember what she said about the tern eggs. She didn't tell me it was an accident, either.

She said he was sorry afterwards. She was in bed for two months, and they gave her too much medicine, enough that she wasn't really herself for almost a year after. The whole time, she said, he was good to her. He was kind. They never fought about money again. She never went to the lake house again, because of the stairs.

He hired a girl to care for her. He bought her a cane with an ivory handle shaped like a marten, because she's descended from the line of the Marten from Higo. Other women envied her such a kind husband, such a patient one, such a calm one.

But she couldn't go to the lake house anymore, and I think he pushed her.

Vi In Yee drained her flask and snuffed out her candle with the flat of her hand. In the darkness, the silence waited, growing heavier with every moment that passed.

Chih couldn't quite get their breath. Their hands were

NGHI VO

pressed over their heart, and they could feel its thunderous beat, and the tears that never seemed so far away stung their eyes and nose.

No, they couldn't have. Of course they couldn't have.

Of course they could have.

"Well," Ru said thinly. "Thank you for your story, Corporal—"

"No."

Tui In Hao rose from her place, the storm come at last, and her face was twisted with fury.

"I want that story struck from the records at once," she said. "Our grandmother loved her husband. She cried for him for a week before she died. What my sister spoke of is certainly not true."

"I beg your pardon, advocate," Ru said, their voice making it clear they were doing no such thing, "but that is impossible. That is not the function of this gathering, nor is it within the ability of the neixin to forget things they have heard and witnessed."

"We might as well be men, if we forgot," called Almost Brilliant. "And advocate, we are not men."

Tui In Hao's eyes snapped up to the rafters, and then she turned back to Ru.

"This is absurd. There is no record that cannot be amended and made correct."

"Everything you have said will be remembered as well," Ru continued.

"But will it be given the same weight, the same importance?"

"This is history, not litigation. That is to say, advocate, this is our world, and not yours."

"Change the record," Tui In Hao insisted, and Ru smiled.

"Under no circumstances."

There was a moment when Chih thought that Tui In Hao would actually draw her sword, and their first thought was *I don't know what to do if that happens*. They didn't. This wasn't some tavern scuffle or dockside fight. This was Singing Hills, and if they didn't litigate, neither did they brawl.

Then Tui In Hao spun on her heel, calling her people to her side. As she went by, she seized her sister's arm, dragging her to her feet and pulling her along despite her protests. Then they were gone, leaving the hall in near darkness, and Ru rose after them, their face grim.

"The doors," they said. "We must get them bolted."

There was a rush of feet to the doors, and above, a tempest of wings, the nexin taking flight. Chih, seated with the attendants, was at the rear of the crowd, but they hurried along behind them as well. They had barely made it out the door before a feathery weight landed on their shoulder and sharp claws pierced their robe.

"Myriad Virtues!" cried Almost Brilliant. "We have left her behind."

There was a moment, unforgivable and shameful, where Chih wanted to tell Almost Brilliant to wait. Myriad Virtues was not hurt. She was not in danger, any more than all of them were. Hadn't Almost Brilliant seen the look on Tui In Hao's face? It was rage, and—

Abruptly the image struck, a little old woman who had lost the most important person in the world to her, unable to walk and left in a dark room with a single candle burning. Shame scalded Chih's cheeks, and they were grateful that one of the first things Singing Hills and Cleric Thien had taught them was to pause before they spoke.

"Of course, forgive me," they said, turning hurriedly.

Almost Brilliant gave them an absent peck to their temple, but she was too distracted to do more as they went back into the hall, too worried for her great-aunt.

Chih's heart nearly broke when they saw Myriad Virtues where they had left her, still perched next to a plate of untouched food and a cup of undrunk wine. She gazed into the flicker of the candle flame, unmoving, as patient as the dead.

People, but not human, Chih thought with a pang, and they knelt beside Myriad Virtues, their hands folded respectfully in front of them.

"Myriad Virtues, we should return you to the aviary. It may not be safe—"

"I must speak," she said without turning to look at

Chih. "Oh, Cleric Chih, grand-niece, I must speak, but I do not know how."

"Of course you know how," said Almost Brilliant timidly. "We are neixin, it is what we—"

"Not our own," Myriad Virtues said, and if she had hands, she would have wrung them. Her wings fanned out briefly instead, displaying the bluntly cut feathers, and Chih stifled a flinch before she folded them back along her body.

Chih didn't know what to do, but then they glanced up the hall, past Ru's seat to the screen and what lay behind it.

Of course they did.

"I would be honored to hear your story, Myriad Virtues," they said as they had said many, many times before. "Whether it is long or short, broken or whole, sad or joyful or angry or strange, I want to hear, and Almost Brilliant, your grand-niece, wants to remember it. Won't you please tell it to us?"

Then they shut their mouth and waited, and after what felt like a small eternity, Myriad Virtues began to speak, her tone halting, her words uncertain.

How strange life is, and how long.

Many years ago, Cleric Thien and I traveled to the capital, and from there we sailed east for a month or more, across water that was as flat as a mirror and water that rose up as tall as the immortal pines, threatening to drown us with every wave. We came at last to the great city of Boddo, the honey city, with its towers that sing like our hills do and where a council of sorceresses rules. It is such a wonderful place, and we stayed at the university there for three years until the old Divine called us home at last.

One day, we went into the underground marketplace, and as Cleric Thien bargained for lunch for themself and a bark cup of mealworms for me, I saw in a cage a hoopoe. At first I was alarmed, for I thought it was a neixin like myself, trapped and imprisoned there due to error or evil. It has happened before, and it might happen again, so we warn our babies. You must warn yours, Almost Brilliant, about how terrible the world might be.

I looked through the wicker bars of the aviary, and I saw a face just like mine, eyes bright like mine were and stripes as bold as mine were back then. I called to her, asking her name and her line, begging her to answer me if she could, but there was no response, and I knew that she was not like me after all, only a bird, only a chirping, hooting thing that could not understand why it was in a cage and had been denied the sky and the water.

Cleric Thien marked my dismay, and they spoke to the vendor, a sturdy boy of thirteen or so. He told us that she had been taken from the plains upriver, caught in his net, and that she would make a fine pet for a lady with her bold colors and bright eyes.

For my sake, Cleric Thien bought her, and begging off our duties at the university, we took a ferry inland, to where the boy had caught her. On either side of the river lies the desert, hot and angry and impassable to all save a few. Akushla itself is a river valley, cut deep and wide into the continent, so they say, by the sword of the North Star as he battled the river horse.

When we let her out, she sat on the ground for a moment as if stunned or perhaps afraid. I did not want to get too close to her, and we watched her until finally she gathered her wits together to fly away.

"Do you want to go with her, join the rest of your family?" teased Cleric Thien.

"Poor taste, cleric. I am not a beast, I am a neixin of Singing Hills," I said, standing upon my dignity.

"Oh?" he asked, still teasing. "Where did the neixin come from, then, if not some riverine land like this one?"

So as we waited for the ferry to return, next to two hyenas who were pretending badly to be people and a family of weavers from the river's heart, I told him.

When the first clerics of Singing Hills were driven from the east, they carried so many books with them that they could not carry food, and so they starved. A family of hoopoes came upon them, and such was their pity that they picked up the books for them. Thus they became the first neixin, with our ability to carry libraries in our hearts.

Long ago, two women argued over how best to keep

their stories, whether it was better to write them down or to remember. The Lady of the Thousand Hands had a mischievous younger brother, who they called the Little Blue, and he overheard this quarrel. Little Blue turned one into a neixin who could remember the world past its beginning and its end, and he turned the other into a cleric with ink on their fingers.

There was once a warlord descended from tigers who could only see the next battle and the next battle and the one after that. The warlord laid to waste a city ruled by a wise princess, who prayed to the three-eyed god that the warlord would remember everything he had done, every life he had taken, every cry for mercy he had ignored. The three-eyed god turned her into the first neixin, who flew after the warlord, singing of his deeds. After that, the warlord gave up the sword and became the first Divine of the order, not in Singing Hills or in Tsu, but in the faraway Copper Kingdom, which came after the Jade Kingdom and the Water Kingdom.

All this and more I told him, because we are told more than a hundred stories about how the neixin came to be, and why. We are valued for our wings and our speech, but our memories are what we are. We are there so that the clerics we love aren't lost, what they've learned and, in some cases, what they died for. We're the memory of their last moments, and we will never forget.

"But you must see," I said, "no matter what the story, we are not beasts. And even if we did not have these stories, which tell us who we are and what we might be, we still would not be. To hear of people who can speak and love and reason and to still think that they are beasts, why, only a man could do that."

Cleric Thien was silent a long time after that, all the way back to our apartment at the university. They were silent as the attendant brought us our evening meal; they were silent as they bathed and made their obeisance to Gentleman Bell.

Finally, before we slept, them in their bed and I in the niche in the wall they had hollowed out just for me, they spoke.

"Forgive me," they said, and from my place, I laughed.

"Of course I will forgive you. Only a beast cannot forgive."

We are not beasts, and I know this because no goat grieves as I do. No raven will have her own wings cut so she can no longer fly. No crocodile will bear a wound because it is better than forgetting.

I wish I were a beast.

Chih sat in the silence afterwards, and then, when they were certain that Myriad Virtues was done, they carefully snuffed out her candle.

"Thank you for your story, Myriad Virtues. When I return to my room, I will write it down and see that it is entered into the archives."

"I'll remember it forever," Almost Brilliant said, alighting next to her great-aunt and fluffing up as round as a ball.

Myriad Virtues was silent, and whatever her oildrop eyes saw, Chih thought it was not the dark hall, now only illuminated by the pillar candles.

"I should take you back to the aviary," Chih said when she would not speak, but Almost Brilliant shook her head.

"Bring her instead to Cleric Thien's rooms," she said. "And some food and water as well, please."

Chih saw them both settled in Cleric Thien's room, Myriad Virtues still silent, and before they could ask if they should stay, Almost Brilliant walked them firmly out.

"Is she going to be all right?" Chih asked at the door.

"No. I don't think so." And then, as if thinking she had been too blunt, she flew from Chih's right shoulder to the left and then back again.

"It has been so much," she said. "She will do better with some rest, and away from the aviary. They have not been very kind to her, though I am sure they think they have."

"I'm glad she has you. I'm glad I have you too."

Almost Brilliant pecked lovingly at their cheek, and it struck Chih how gentle the neixin were when they did that. Their beaks were designed to dig grubs out of hard earth and wood, and Chih's cheek was certainly softer than either.

"I am glad you are glad," Almost Brilliant said. "Now try to remember that when next I tell you you need to be nicer to the local magistrates or that you do not need to spend all our money on sesame brittle."

Despite everything, Chih's spirit lifted. At some point, maybe not soon, but at some point Almost Brilliant thought they would be fighting about magistrates and sesame brittle again.

"I will," they promised.

They headed to the gate, barred now, and they found Ru at the booth where the novices on door duty sat, massaging their foot with a blank look on their face.

"How is it?" Chih asked, leaning against the wall next to them.

"Quiet. There was some shouting earlier, but everyone's gone to sleep now, I think. Where have you been?"

"Myriad Virtues. She wanted to tell her story too, so I sat with Almost Brilliant. It was a good story."

Ru frowned, and Chih braced themself for a fight, but they only shrugged, nodding.

"It has been very difficult for her. I don't think I've seen any neixin be so grieved when their cleric died."

"She and Cleric Thien had something special. Almost Brilliant is with her now."

"That's good." Chih glanced up at the main gate. The small gate could be sealed with iron bars, rendered impassable if necessary, but in some ways, the main gate was less secure. It was barred with treated timbers reinforced with bands of iron, but against two mammoths—

"Are you going to go to bed?" Chih asked. "You can't make the gate stronger by staring at it."

"But what if I could?" Ru joked weakly, but they shrugged. "I'm staying."

Chih took a seat at the base of the wall, leaned up against the stone. In the dry months, the stone held the heat all night. This late in the year, there was already a dampness seeping through their formal robes to their skin.

"All right. Wake me when we're ready to go sleep in our beds like sensible people."

Ru snorted, but they reached down to take Chih's hand.

Overhead, the stars turned, and Chih closed their eyes.

Chapter Nine

Chih dreamed of being a child again, following along behind Cleric Thien as they walked the river path.

"Keep up," Cleric Thien said, not turning around. "We're almost home."

Somehow, Chih knew they were not. The path was wrong, the light off the water was wrong, and there was something wrong with Cleric Thien as well. Chih stared at Cleric Thien's back as they walked, an unease gripping their belly and climbing up their spine.

Suddenly Cleric Thien stopped, and Chih realized what was wrong.

Where is Myriad Virtues?

Cleric Thien turned towards them, and Chih went to take a step back only to find their legs heavy, so heavy, as if they were weighed down with molten lead.

"I can see you," Cleric Thien said in a slow and tarry voice, and then the world ended with a boom.

Chih was on their feet before they remembered that they had fallen asleep sitting up. They got briefly tangled in their long formal robes before they righted themself, and the sound came again, a thunderous crash that they felt straight to their bones.

Ru snatched up their cane, cursing the whole while, stumbling briefly as their foot refused to support them. Chih stepped forward to let Ru catch at their shoulder, staying still until Ru steadied and got their cane positioned to support them.

"Light them!" Ru bellowed, their voice carrying over the crash, and out of the corner of their eye Chih saw motion from the walkway over the gates. When they squinted up into the dawning sky, they could see a handful of novices lighting up braziers that almost immediately billowed a dirty gray smoke. The smoke rose up only to be fanned towards the gate. Chih recognized the leaf-shaped straw fans, as long as their arm, that were sold along the river all summer.

They started to ask what was going on, but then they got a whiff of the smoke and gagged. It was a dense stench, barnyard animals and river mud with a hard sting that got into their nose and their eyes. They started to cry out, but Ru was handing them a cloth, their own face already covered entirely below the eyes.

"Cover up," Ru said. "And come on. I need to get above the gate."

The staircase leading up to the walkway was narrow with no handrail, the stairs steep and curved in the middle. There was just barely enough space for Chih and Ru to ascend, Ru's free hand on Chih's shoulder for balance and their cane providing support.

They emerged into the light just as the wind turned, blowing the smoke back towards the abbey, making the masked novices who tended the fires choke.

"Snuff them," Ru shouted, and they covered the braziers with the solid lids, closing the smoke up and suffocating the fire.

"What in the world," coughed Chih.

"Dried horse dung mixed with about a year's supply of dried chili peppers. It stings like scorpions," Ru replied, but they were looking over the edge of the parapet.

The humans had figured out the trick pretty quickly, pulling scarves over their faces, but the mammoths looked incensed. Sho swung her trunk back to wipe at her eyes, swaying back and forth with dismay, her rider trying helplessly to calm her. Bibi had knelt and was rubbing her face in the dirt, bent down so far that Vi In Yee had to hook her knee around her saddle horn to stay seated.

"Where'd you learn that?"

"The archives, of course. I was hoping they'd forgotten that trick. Most of the places the mammoths march don't have peppers like that."

Below, Vi In Yee was shouting, and she slithered forward, her foot hooked around the horn now, to pour

water from her flask into Bibi's eyes. Someone was trying to do the same for Sho, but she shook her enormous
head, and the person with the flask had to skip back or
get flattened.

Chih yelped at a flutter by their head, Cleverness
Himself breezing past them to land on the stone.

"Well?" he demanded, and Ru nodded.

"Try it," they said. "Only be care—"

Cleverness Himself was gone before Ru finished
speaking, and Ru swore instead, low and inventive and
furious as a dozen neixin swept from the walls towards
the mammoths. Chih stared as the birds dove straight for
the two mammoths, their wings whirring as they fell almost straight down.

There was absolutely no precision about it, nothing more than a storm of black and white wings flying
straight for the mammoths' faces and the faces of their
riders. The neixin were small, but no one liked getting
hit by a flurry of feathers and claws to the face, and as
Chih had noted the night before, those beaks could be
impressively painful.

"They're going to get flattened," Chih gasped.

"About half the aviary agrees with you, and they're
preparing to fly for Tsu with news of what happened if
the mammoths really do break the gates and trample the
archives," Ru said. "The half that doesn't agree is down
there right now."

For a moment, just a moment, Chih thought it might have worked. Sho, at her rider's urging, backed away from the scene, but then inexperienced Bibi trumpeted, a shrieking bellow that that drilled into Chih's ears, that filled the world with its fury. From below, they heard distinctly Vi In Yee's single "fuck," and then the stones shook as the mammoth reared back and then slammed into the gate. There was no restraint this time, no precision war machine directed by a rider.

While Sho stood with her four feet planted, Bibi was maddened by the neixin, and the gate bore the brunt of her wrath. Two more heavy blows bent the wood in, and then she simply put one massive shoulder to the wood and shoved.

The ancient hinges tore with a pained metallic shriek, and then the gate splintered and cracked, buckling before falling entirely to Bibi's trampling feet. Now she was under the shelter of the wall, harder for the neixin to reach, and she trumpeted angrily, swinging her trunk back and forth and, as Chih watched in horror, knocking one neixin tumbling.

That neixin narrowly avoided hitting the wall and instead flew upward, straight into Chih's hands, panting and giggling.

"Did you see me?" Chiep demanded. "Did you see, Cleric Chih? I almost got her *eye*."

"I did," Chih said, taking a firmer hold on Chiep,

because if Almost Brilliant found out they'd let Chiep go fight a mammoth, their friendship would probably never recover.

Fortunately, Chiep didn't seem inclined to fly back into the fray, and it was only then that Chih realized that a strange hush had fallen.

Despite the gate being down, the northerners didn't come through it, and all of the abbey's defenders were staring at the single figure at the center of the courtyard.

It was a cleric with a neixin on their shoulder, their hands tucked into the sleeves of their indigo robe. They stood as straight as a spear, and their shaved head was tilted in gentle curiosity, as if they were only listening to a good story.

"Ma!" Chiep said in surprise.

"*Cleric Thien,*" said Ru through a mouth that didn't seem to work right, and the cleric waited for them patiently in the dawning day.

Chapter Ten

They ended up in the Divine's receiving hall, a pleasant room with shutters that could be thrown open to let in the dawn light. Ru and Chih knelt on one side of the hall with Vi In Yee and Tui In Hao across from them. Absently, Chih noted that Vi In Yee looked as if she was still drunk and rather massively embarrassed, if her red face and too-straight posture were anything to go by. Tui In Hao's face was a mask, and she only had eyes for the figure that was, right or wrong, seated at the head of the hall in the place reserved for the most senior cleric.

It was Cleric Thien's face and form, of that there could be no doubt. Echo spirits could only be heard, not seen, and no walking ghost could enter the abbey undetected and steal Cleric Thien's shape.

More than that, however, it was the way the cleric knelt, as calm as stone and as patient, their hands laid flat and neat on their thighs, their eyes slightly squinted to account for the astigmatism that had bothered them almost as long as Chih and Ru had been alive.

"What in the four hells," Vi In Yee said finally. "We were told you were dead."

"Our grandfather is dead," Tui In Hao said through gritted teeth. "That is not the kind of mistake Singing Hills would make, *is* it, acting Divine."

"Anyone may make a mistake," Ru said calmly, and only Chih knew them well enough to hear the faint tremor in their voice. "But I am not the one who can supply answers here. Almost Brilliant?"

Almost Brilliant shifted on the cleric's shoulder. She held her head proudly high, and she surveyed her audience.

"My great-aunt Myriad Virtues was grieved to death by the loss of her companion, the Cleric Thien. As days turned to nights and pushed her ever further from the last moment they were together, all she wanted to do was to forget her grief, but of course that is something no neixin can do. So she stopped being a neixin."

"If you can't grieve, can't fly, can't remember, why, you might as well be a man," Chih said without thinking, and suddenly they felt the weight of Tui In Hao's eyes on them. Her gaze was as heavy as the law itself, but when she spoke, her voice was slow and thoughtful.

"A few nights ago, I went walking in the dusk. I wanted to gather my thoughts, to remember why it was that I had left home and come so far south for a man I had never met, whose honor and duty to the Coh of Northern Bell Pass was fulfilled before I was born.

"I wanted to be alone, so I was angry when a bird came to me in the shadow of your walls, small and dull, insignificant in every way. She asked me for a favor, to clip the flight feathers of her wings to the quick, and even in my frustration I was shocked. I asked her why she would do such a thing.

"For grief, she said. *For sorrow. When the world has changed so completely, why should I remain the same? I cannot remain. I cannot stay."*

Tui In Hao took a measured breath, as if she was about to make her final argument to the judges.

"I did as she asked, and she went on her way. I put it out of my mind, but I dreamed of her again, that little bird, shedding who she was so she might survive better. Sometimes, you cannot survive and still be who you were."

"Almost never, I think," Ru murmured.

"So who are you, then?" demanded Vi In Yee, addressing the cleric at the head of the table. "We know who you look like. Who are you now?"

At the head of the room, the cleric blinked peaceably. They reached up to touch their seamed face, the round flat nose, their lips thin from being pressed together against irritation or laughter, and then they brushed Almost Brilliant away. She fluttered hesitantly for a moment and then flew to Chih's shoulder, her nails digging in fretfully.

"I am no longer Myriad Virtues," they said.

Chih could see the shape of it now, transformation fueled by grief. In the stories that Myriad Virtues had told Cleric Thien so long ago in Boddo, just a fraction of the explanations for the origin of the neixin, that was always the way of it. Great love or great passion or great vengeance had created the neixin, so perhaps it stood to reason that great sorrow could change them again.

"I am what remains of Cleric Thien in this world," they continued with measured patience. "I am every moment they have walked within these walls, from the day they crossed the gates you have knocked down to the night they breathed their last in the infirmary, calling for the novices they taught and the wife they left behind decades ago."

They smiled.

"I am a thousand stories of Northern Bell Pass, and an illustrious career in the capital, of a northern tribunal tricked. I am a father and a grandfather as well as a cleric, because no single thing takes away from the rest."

Tui In Hao's fingers tapped restlessly on the handle of the sword laid by her side. When she spoke, however, her voice was tentative.

"The story my sister told at the banquet. Our grandmother's fall. What is the truth?"

The cleric's head dropped, and at first Chih thought it was because they did not know, but then they realized it was for sorrow.

"I pushed her. I was angry. I never intended for her to be hurt, but as you and I both know, advocate, intent never excuses the outcome. That moment lives inside me, always, on my best and brightest days, and even if I did not have a heart of myriad virtues, I will not forget."

Every moment, Chih couldn't help but think. *When they taught us to read, when they saw me introduced to Almost Brilliant, when we left home for the first time.*

The cleric tilted their head, looking at Tui In Hao.

"And what do you think would be justice for that, granddaughter?"

Tui In Hao bristled, and Chih wondered if it was too much, the transformed neixin claiming her as if it was their right, but then she shook her head.

"It would have been her right to call you to court within five years of the incident. You might have forfeited half your family holdings to her. You might have lost the hand that pushed her. Nothing can be done now."

"That is punishment, where the law excels," said the cleric. "Justice is a more difficult thing."

"She died calling for you," Tui In Hao said stiffly. She could speak of honor and legal rights with ease. This was more difficult. "She didn't know where you were, and she forgot that you had gone. She called your name over and over again."

She struggled for a moment.

"She *missed* you."

"Then I shall come."

Chih and Ru stared, Vi In Yee looked as if she had no idea that things could get this strange, but Tui In Hao bared her teeth.

"And what are you?" she demanded. "A thousand stories told over and over again until they are only words."

Chih took a deep breath, aware of Tui In Hao's sword, of the mammoths at the gates and how badly this could still go.

"I beg your pardon, advocate," they said in their humblest voice, "but what was your grandfather to you but a thousand stories told over and over again?"

Tui In Hao hesitated, and Vi In Yee put her hand over her sister's.

"That's all he ever was to us, and you know it, sis. And Grandma, she remembered a living man, didn't she? Why not have a living man to tend her grave and sing to her spirit? It's better than bones."

"Better than bones," Tui In Hao repeated, and then she passed her hand over her eyes. When she looked up, however, her face was resolute.

"Come tend her grave, come sing her the songs she liked best, and drink to her final long night. If you will do this, then I will consider all matters settled with Singing Hills."

Chih knew that Ru wanted to protest, and they did too. It was like losing Cleric Thien twice. On their shoulder, Almost Brilliant's breath hitched, because they had lost Myriad Virtues as well.

Cleric Thien glanced at them, love and adoration and a touch of exasperation all at once.

"We have taught you well, haven't we? We have told you again and again that the world is strange."

And then to Tui In Hao, "Thank you, granddaughter. I will come, and I will honor Myat Ly Ung."

The northern delegation left the next morning, a palanquin secured for Cleric Thien. Before they had dropped the woven blinds, they had pressed their cheek to Ru's face and then Chih's.

"You will be fine," they said. "I love you both."

It was more of a goodbye than Chih had any right to expect, and they hadn't cried nearly as much as they were afraid they were going to.

Now the mammoths were pawing at the ground, ready to be on their way, and Chih went to say goodbye to Vi In Yee.

"Is this the right thing?" Chih found themself asking, and Vi In Yee gave them a crooked smile.

"Bit late to start having doubts now, cleric. But I think my sister and I have the solace we wanted for our grandmother's spirit, and you have a dead man to bury, so that's the end of it."

"Not a man, a cleric," Chih corrected, as they had been itching to do for days, and Vi In Yee nodded, chagrined.

"Sorry, I'll remember. How much trouble are you and the other one going to be in when the folks in charge get back?"

"Maybe some, but Singing Hills has always been a practical sort of place. Debates are passed down like treasured antiques. They'll probably be fighting over whether we did the right thing or whether there was even a right thing to do in this situation for ages. Maybe Cleric Thien would care to write back and give us their opinion."

"Weird folks," Vi In Yee said, shaking her head. "Anyway, thanks for the smoke bomb recipe. We never should have lost track of that one."

"It's what we're here for. Thank you for paying for the gate repair."

"Bibi's temperamental, and I was drunk. No excuse, though." She paused awkwardly.

"You know we never would have done it, right? I didn't want to knock down your gate, and we wouldn't have gone after your archives. Tui-ah said we were just going to scare you a little."

"We couldn't know that," Chih said as calmly as they could. "We have a long history, and there have been both wartime Divines and pilgrim Divines. We've had to fight and to flee, and that doesn't happen if people *don't* want to trample you and everything that's important to you."

"Yeah, I'm sorry about that too." Vi In Yee clapped Chih on the shoulder. "If you're ever in Northern Bell Pass, come look me up. Lots of good stories up that way."

Chih probably would someday.

Ru and Tui In Hao were completing their far more formal farewell, and then Tui In Hao climbed up onto Bibi's back behind her sister. Her gaze was fixed on the north, but Vi In Yee waved before she called for Bibi to turn and march.

Chih and Ru watched through the broken gates as the northern delegation started off. The neixin observed all of this from the wall, and then three broke off from the rest and glided down to where they stood, Almost Brilliant to Chih's shoulder, and Chiep and Cleverness Himself crowded together on one of Ru's.

"How exciting that was!" Chiep exclaimed. "What does it mean? What's going to happen next?"

"What happens next is that you will wait and see," said Almost Brilliant.

"Probably something weird," said Cleverness Himself, and Chiep snuggled under his wing.

"You always say that, Baba."

Ru and Chih both managed to miss a step while standing still.

"Baba?" asked Chih finally.

"We do have a lot of catching up to do," Almost Brilliant said demurely. "And acting Divine, if you didn't notice, perhaps that means you need to work harder on your observational skills."

"I'll take that under advisement," Ru said as Cleverness Himself looked far too pleased with the entire situation.

The nexin lifted off the wall, a flight of birds wheeling overhead before returning home to work and talk and eat, and Cleverness Himself and Chiep flew to join them. Almost Brilliant nuzzled Chih's cheek briefly.

"I mean that, by the way. We have a lot of catching up to do. Perhaps we can do it as we get your travel records entered into the archives properly."

"Ugh. I was hoping that someone else might—"

"No, you," said Almost Brilliant sternly. "No putting it off on some poor novice that you bribed with candy."

"She's right," Ru said, eyes laughing. "It'll be more accurate if you enter the work yourself."

"You're boring now," Chih said. "Did you know that? You are so boring."

"But I'll also help, and we can eat the candy ourselves. How's that?"

"Fine. I guess I'm home after all."

Even as they said it, Chih knew they were. Maybe not for how long, or what home really was now with Ru in charge and Cleric Thien and Myriad Virtues gone, but it was still home.

They followed Ru to the archives as the wind picked up, whistling through the hollow places that pocked the stony land. The sound was eerie if you weren't used to it like Chih and Ru were, a moaning, sighing whistle, and as the hills sang, the first drops of rain fell from the darkening sky.

Acknowledgments

So a few years ago, I headed over to Waukegan to help my best friend clear out her uncle's house. I couldn't attend the funeral (fuck you very much, covid), but I spent a few weekends helping Carolyn sort and haul. Anyone who's done this sort of work knows how weird it is, sad and fascinating and frustrating and funny at strange times in irregular measures. Uncle Bill left behind a house, a neurotic sheltie named Otto, and all the bits and pieces that come from being a pretty cool guy with several decades' worth of hobbies.

Carolyn and her husband, Cris, kept the sheltie, I kept a card advertising *mustache rides 5¢,* and along the way I found the best thing. Tucked in a side table in the basement, underneath the whiskey bottle shaped like a water tower (it had a tiny spigot for the whiskey to come out, super cool), I found this picture of Carolyn from when she was a kid. At the age of six, she had the same big smile and the same big brown eyes that she has now, and it's just awesome. I bet her uncle thought so too.

Sitting in the basement, keeping an eye out for the wolf spider that had been menacing me all weekend, I thought about love and how we leave it in weird places for ourselves and for others to find. Some of that went into writing *Mammoths at the Gates*. Hope you liked it.

So this is Singing Hills number four, and like every single one of these books, it wouldn't exist without the efforts of a lot of very wonderful people. Thanks are very much due to my agent, Diana Fox, who really made me think about the neixin as magical black boxes (still recovering from that, honestly), and my editor, Ruoxi Chen, whose keen eye has kept me from a number of shipwrecks.

Thanks as well go to the hardworking and brilliant team at Tordotcom Publishing, including Oliver Dougherty and Irene Gallo in editorial; Lauren Hougen, Jim Kapp, Greg Collins, Amanda Hong, and Kyle Avery in production; Alexis Saarela, Michael Dudding, and Samantha Friedlander in publicity; and Christine Foltzer and Jess Kiley in art. Thank you as well to Alyssa Winans for her knockout cover.

Thank you to Cris Chingwa, Victoria Coy, Leah Kolman, Amy Lepke, and Meredy Shipp, 'cause we have such a good time.

And Shane Hochstetler, Grace Palmer, and Carolyn Mulroney, I adore you all, and can one of you guys come pick me up? I lost my transit card, and I don't wanna walk home in the rain.

As for everyone reading, thank you to you guys as well. Hope you're having a good time out there, stay safe, be kind, drink some water!